SOARING FREE

Club of Dominance 6

Becca Van

MENAGE EVERLASTING

Siren Publishing, Inc.
www.SirenPublishing.com

A SIREN PUBLISHING BOOK
IMPRINT: Ménage Everlasting

SOARING FREE
Copyright © 2015 by Becca Van

ISBN: 978-1-63259-649-9

First Printing: July 2015

Cover design by Les Byerley
All art and logo copyright © 2015 by Siren Publishing, Inc.

Printed in the U.S.A.

PUBLISHER
Siren Publishing, Inc.
www.SirenPublishing.com

SOARING FREE

Club of Dominance 6

BECCA VAN

Prologue

He'd been watching her for months now. She was so damn beautiful and he knew she was meant to be his. Paul hated that he only caught a glimpse of her every now and then, when she was going to work.

Because she worked odd hours, he often stayed up just so he could watch her come home. She had the lightest blonde hair he'd ever seen and he wondered if it felt as soft as it looked.

Joni always wore nice clothes. Not like the whores who liked to display every bit of flesh they could without being totally indecent. She only left the two top buttons on her shirt undone without a hint of cleavage and although the pants or skirts she wore were mostly black and looser than he would have liked, they molded her hips and ass to perfection. She wasn't a tall woman. In fact she was downright petite compared to him, but she had the sexiest body and he couldn't wait to get his hands on her. He could just imagine her moaning as he caressed her bare skin and licked her all over.

Whenever they met in their daily routines, which were nowhere near enough, she acted so shy and demure. Paul needed to spend more time with her so she would get to know him and eventually go out with him. If he could find out where she worked, he could somehow wrangle his way into her workplace and keep an eye on her.

Rage filled him at the thought of another man touching what was his and he clenched his fists.

He had a few weeks of vacation time owed to him so he decided he would put in for it first thing tomorrow. Then he would spend his time following and watching and then he'd make his move.

She was meant for him and he wasn't letting her escape. They would be perfect together and he wasn't going to let anything or anyone get in the way of their destiny.

Chapter One

Joni looked around her in wide-eyed astonishment and wondered if she'd done the right thing by agreeing to come to this den of iniquity. She couldn't help but cringe each time she heard the slap of one of those small whips hitting flesh or the cries of pain coming from the woman tethered to the weird-looking *X* contraption.

She glanced over at Kara and tried to smile but she wasn't sure she had pulled that action off when her new friend frowned at her and started to make her way closer to her.

"Are you okay?" Kara asked, placing a comforting hand on her shoulder.

Joni wanted to tell her no and that she was leaving, but she couldn't quite make herself utter the words lodged in her throat, so she nodded instead.

"I promise you that all the people being…hit have consented."

Joni met Kara's eyes and then looked to either side of her when Kara's men, Doctors Nathan and Nixon Charleston, came to stand on either side of her. She'd met Kara when she'd gone to their doctor's office with a bout of the flu and she and Kara had hit it off. That had been six months ago, and now she and Kara met every Friday lunchtime for food and coffee.

When Kara had invited her for a night out at a club she'd never envisioned something like this.

Joni felt so far out of her element she couldn't stay still, and even though she was sort of shocked by what was going on around her, she was also intrigued. She wanted to know why people would let someone else inflict pain on them. What bothered her most, though, was the fact she was getting turned on. It wasn't the nakedness that ramped up her libido but the cries of ecstasy she could hear every now and then.

"Do you do this?" Joni asked and then wished the floor would open up and swallow her whole. She wished she could retract her question but since she'd blurted it out, she waited for an answer. She just hoped her face wasn't as red as it felt.

"Yes."

"Why?" Joni gulped as she swallowed and nearly choked on her own saliva. She really wished she could hold her tongue.

"I know you don't understand, but having impact play makes endorphins surge through the body and warms the skin. Your body ends up being so much more sensitive and when you come it's…out of this world."

"You can…" Joni did bite her tongue this time. She bit it so hard she tasted blood.

"It's really hard to explain if you haven't experienced it before." Nixon eyed her over the top of his glass before taking a sip of his drink.

"It's a freeing experience for a sub to be tied up and spanked or flogged. Just knowing you can't move or control what's about to happen, can be very liberating," Nathan said.

"If you say so." Joni sipped her white wine and swished it around her mouth to rid herself of the coppery taste of the blood still lingering on her tongue before she swallowed. She mentally shrugged over what they'd told her. It wasn't that she was judging what others needed or wanted to feel more, but she knew this sort of thing wasn't for her.

So why are you horny? Shut the fuck up!

Her life was all about control and there was no way she would ever relinquish her body to someone to beat on her. *Been there done that. Not ever doing that again.*

* * * *

Thomas stared at the monitor and watched as the blonde shifted from foot to foot again. She looked so uncomfortable but her gaze kept going back to the raised dais as Turner and Barry flogged and spanked Charlie. The expressions flitting across her face were adorable and he wanted to race down the stairs, pull her into his arms, and offer her comfort but he knew she wouldn't accept any overtures from a stranger.

He zoomed in on her face and body and saw that her nipples were hard and pushing against the material of her blue shirt, but he could tell she didn't want to be turned on. Thomas was glad he had audio as well because when he heard Charlie's scream of ecstasy he watched the blonde's reaction more intently. Her whole body quivered like a shiver had just raced up her spine and her lips parted as she drew in a deep breath. He watched her pink tongue slide out from between her lips and she licked over them before taking a gulp from her wine glass.

He wished he could hear what she said when she spoke to Kara, but all he could hear were cries from other patrons getting off or screams of pained pleasure as they were played with, plus the babble of other conversations going on drowned out her voice.

Tom zoomed out again and searched the club hoping to see his housemates and good friends Gabe Solar and Nic Flange. The three of them owned a pub between them but since they had such great and loyal employees, they had plenty of spare time on their hands.

Tom had been a security guard ever since he'd turned eighteen. A few years ago, he was headhunted by Turner, Barry, and Tank. He was glad because he loved working at the Club of Dominance. He, Nic, and Gabe came here whenever they wanted to socialize and have a drink with their friends.

He'd met Gabe and Nic when they had started working at the same security company over ten years ago and they had hit it off.

When the opportunity had arisen to buy, first a house, and then the pub between the three of them, they had pooled their cash and bought both. They hadn't looked back since.

Although Thomas loved the pub he missed the security aspect and when Turner had approached him to keep an eye on things, he'd jumped at the chance. And right now he was very glad he had.

He, Gabe, and Nic were also Doms and even though they'd played with a few subs at the Club of Dominance, playing with different women had gotten old real quick.

They were good friends with all the Doms of the club and as he watched his buddies find love, he got more and more envious.

About six months ago he'd sat at the kitchen table with Gabe and Nic, telling them he wanted a woman he could wake up to every morning and had been relieved when they'd agreed. And although he'd been exuberant at first, he'd begun to think they'd never find a woman for their own.

But as he eyed the blonde standing close to Kara he had a feeling their search was over. First things first, though. He needed to know if his friends were as drawn to her as he was, and if so, they needed to meet her. For all he knew she was already in a relationship and if he was unlucky she might not even be into men.

Tom drew his cell phone from his pocket as he searched the crowd and when he spotted Gabe and Nic watching a scene unfold in one of the rooms on the other side of the club, he hit speed dial.

"Yo," Nic answered with his usual greeting.

"I need you and Gabe to head over to the bar," Tom said.

"Why? Is there trouble brewing?" Nic asked.

"No trouble but there is one hell of a woman talking to Kara and her men."

"Is she a sub?"

"I'm not sure, but from the way she's reacting to what's going on around her, she is lugubriously fascinated."

Tom saw Nic nudge Gabe's arm and then they were both making their way toward the bar.

"What's she wearing?" Nic asked.

"Black jeans and a blue shirt."

As his friends got closer to the bar, Tom heard Nic's indrawn breath and then he whistled quietly in appreciation.

"Damn! She is hot."

"Told ya."

"When are you being relieved?" Nic asked.

"Rowan just entered. I'll be there in a minute."

"Good. We won't approach her until you get here. You want a beer?"

"Yeah, thanks."

"See you in a few."

"That you will." Tom disconnected the call and then he took time to update Rowan. He glanced as his watch and headed toward the door, cursing under his breath when he saw ten minutes had gone by. He was eager to find out who the little blonde was and if she was a sub. His heart was racing in his chest and his hands were sweaty.

Tom took a deep breath, controlling his breathing and trying to get his excitement under wraps. He had a good feeling about this and hoped he was right, but it wouldn't do to get his hopes up too high only to be shot down.

One step at a time, Tom. Don't be too pushy.

He repeated that mantra over and over trying to curtail his enthusiasm. It wouldn't do to scare her off.

* * * *

Joni felt eyes on her but didn't turn to see who was watching. Everywhere those eyes touched, her body tingled and the hair on her nape stood on end, but she determinedly kept her gaze forward. But that was a mistake, too, because she kept looking back to the raised stage where another lot of people were setting up for a "scene."

Kara and her men hadn't stopped explaining what the club was about and the more they told her the more turned on she got. After watching the scene between the blonde and the two Dom owners she realized that the woman wasn't being hurt at all and was actually enjoying everything her men did to her. When the Charlie woman had screamed her orgasm Joni hadn't known where to look. She'd felt like she was invading their privacy, but found her gaze going back to the three people again and again. And the more she watched the hornier she got.

"You're not going to...do that are you?" Joni asked Kara. She didn't know if she could watch her friend and her two men getting intimate. She was scared she would never be able to look Kara in the eye again.

"No. We're just here to socialize tonight," Kara answered.

"Thank God for that," Joni muttered, and when Kara burst out laughing she realized she'd heard her and her face heated up even more.

Kara shoved Nix aside and moved to Joni's side. "Don't you find all this...stimulating?"

Joni licked her dry lips and shook her head but to her surprise she changed the shake to a nod.

Damn it! Stop it!

She gulped the last of her wine and decided it was time she got out of here before she made an even bigger fool of herself.

She turned toward the bar and froze when she saw three tall, muscular men eying her up and down. She spun back to Kara and stood up on tiptoes to whisper in her ear.

"I have to go. I have work tomorrow."

"Joni, don't be scared. No one in here will hurt you," Kara whispered back.

"I–I..."

"None of the men here would ever do to you what your ex did." Kara rubbed Joni on the back.

"You don't know that, Kara."

Kara nodded her head but then changed it to a shake. "I do actually. Everyone in this club is a member or employee. They have to read the rules and sign a contract. Anyone not adhering to the rules is kicked out and never allowed back in."

"You and I both know that men, people, can hide their true personalities."

"Yes they can," Kara said. "But Masters Turner, Barry, and Tank do extensive background searches. They would never let anyone with a criminal record set foot on the first step let alone into the club if they were aggressive, abusive, or had rap sheet."

"Ever heard of false ID?" Joni asked facetiously.

Her ex had played her from the start even giving her a false name and address. She'd fallen for his good looks and charm and after six months of dating he'd moved into her apartment with her.

That was the day he'd begun to change. John had criticized everything about her. Her weight, her clothes, her hair, her body and the day she'd stood up to him and asked him to leave was the day she'd ended up in the hospital. He'd beaten her black and blue, broken a couple of ribs, and then taken off. Joni had spent two weeks in the hospital and had vowed from then on to never get involved with another man again. That had been two years ago and although she'd just turned twenty-five she had her whole life ahead of her. She didn't ever want another man in her life.

"I know John fooled you, Joni, but not all men are like him."

"I know," Joni sighed. "But after what he did to me I just can't go through that again. It would destroy me. He lied to me and whenever he was on a so-called sales trip he was actually with his wife."

"You shouldn't feel guilty about that, honey. He lied to you."

"Yes, he did and because of that and what he did, I have huge trust issues."

"That's understandable, but not every man on this planet is a bigamous abusive asshole. I'm so glad he got his just desserts, though. If you hadn't pressed charges for assault and gone on the witness stand at his trial his poor wife might still be with him."

Joni nodded. She knew Kara was right. She wished she'd known Kara back then. She was a great friend and had helped her come out of her shell, but she still had a long way to go. She'd even seen a counselor and although her confidence had grown, it was nowhere near where it had been before she'd met John. She was just glad her mom would never know how gullible she'd been.

Her mother had died when Joni had turned twenty in a hit-and-run accident and when the cops came knocking on her door months later after searching for her mother's murderer, she'd been shocked to find out her estranged father had killed her. It had taken her a long time to get over the grief and trauma, which had eventually turned to anger. Anger at her father for taking the only person who had ever loved her unconditionally away from her.

It had taken her years to come to terms with the fact she was feeling guilty because she was still alive and then she'd met John, whose real name had turned out to be Angus Peace. He'd lied to her about everything. What his name was, how old he was, and, oh yeah, there was the fact he was married with a couple of kids.

She'd been lying in a hospital bed in pain and so totally wary of everything and then she met Tanya Peace. Tanya had come to see her and make sure she was all right after her husband was arrested.

Joni's first instinct was embarrassed shame and she'd apologized to Tanya, and then she'd found the whole sordid story pouring out of her mouth and she'd cried so much she'd been sick.

Tanya had been absolutely wonderful and thanked Joni for having the courage to press charges against her husband. She'd been dealing with physical and verbal abuse from the cowardly bastard for four years, but hadn't had the courage to call the police or leave.

The teary-eyed woman had said she forgave Joni, although there was nothing to be forgiven for since she'd been had by a con man, and just before she'd left she told Joni she was going to file for divorce, get her kids, and leave town.

Joni had wished her well and, with a wave, Tanya was gone.

She blinked as she came back to the present and realized that Kara was awaiting a response. "I know that not every man is like John was, but I can't do that again."

She swallowed audibly and looked around when she noticed the noise in the club had diminished and realized she had been almost shouting so Kara could hear her. She glanced up at Nix and Nate and quickly looked away when she saw they were staring at her, both of them with frowns on their faces. They'd obviously heard every word she'd said and she wondered if they'd heard the whole conversation or just the last part of it. She shifted from foot to foot and sighed again, but this time with relief when loud music began to play once more.

"I think I should just head on home, Kara." She waved her hand in the air to indicate the club room and continued on. "This just isn't me."

"How do you know that?" a deep tenor said from behind her. "Have you ever tried BDSM?"

Joni's first instinct was to whip her head around to look over her shoulder and see who had spoken, but she forced herself to remain still and not respond.

"Hey, Thomas, Gabe, Nic. How are you doing?"

"Hello, Kara. We're fine. You're looking very sexy tonight."

Joni felt every hair on her body stand up as the new male voice washed over her but she continued to stay still. Every muscle in her body was as tense as a bowstring ready to fire and the urge to look behind her was almost too much to ignore, but she compelled her body to obey her mind.

"Thanks." Kara smiled, and then she reached out to grab hold of Joni's wrist and tugged her next to her before she placed her hands on her shoulders to turn her around.

"Nic, Gabe, Tom, I'd like you to meet a good friend of mine. This is Joni Meeks."

Joni looked up and blinked when all she saw were three broad muscular, material-covered chests before she lifted her gaze up over wide shoulders to meet three pairs of eyes looking at her avidly. She swallowed and nervously licked dry lips, before locking gazes with soulful brown eyes. His dark brown hair was cut short but still long enough to run fingers through. When she saw his Adam's apple move she lowered her gaze and watched the sexy masculine motion and then she met his eyes again.

The man took a step forward and held his hand out to her. "I'm Nicholas Flange but everyone calls me Nic."

"Hello." Joni took the proffered hand and, as soon as her skin touched his, she wanted to draw back, but made herself clasp his hand for an introduction before pulling away. She hated the way her body reacted to his handsome face and sexy body, but there was no way she was going to act on the attraction she felt or let her awareness of him show.

"Pleased to meet you, Joni."

She shifted her gaze to the black-haired man and drew in a deep breath when she met his searching green eyes. "I'm Gabe Solar."

"Hi." Once again Joni had to curb the tingles racing throughout her body as she shook hands with the good-looking man.

She surreptitiously wiped her hand on her jeans and met the hazel eyes of the last man.

"Hi, Joni. I'm Thomas Quentin. You can call me Tom or Quen, whatever you'd prefer."

She gripped Tom's outstretched hand, clasped it, and quickly let go again. "It's nice to meet you all." Joni turned to Kara and glared at her, but when she spoke she made sure to keep her voice calm and modulated. "I have to get going, Kara. I have an early start tomorrow."

"But..." Kara began but Joni interrupted her.

"Thanks for inviting me. I'll see you next Friday," Joni said and, before Kara could say anything else, she turned and hurried toward the exit. She didn't need to look back to know that she was being watched. Nic, Tom, and Gabe had been leaning against the bar earlier watching her, and although she'd been uncomfortable at their perusal, she'd also been flattered.

It didn't matter she was blonde or she had blue eyes. She was passably pretty but wasn't model material. A couple of years ago she may well have started flirting with them, but after John she didn't want attention from the opposite sex ever again.

The pain of his beating had faded but she still remembered the agony she endured from his fists and feet as he'd kicked her, yet it was the shame that she couldn't let go of. She was ashamed of ever falling for such a lying, narcissistic asshole. It didn't matter that her therapist had told her she had nothing to be ashamed or embarrassed about and that it wasn't her fault she'd been abused verbally or physically.

Joni wasn't about to let anyone treat her like that ever again. Even if it meant being alone for the rest of her life.

Chapter Two

"Why is Joni scared of men?" Gabe asked Kara.

Kara glanced at Nixon and Nate before meeting Gabe's eyes again. "I'm sorry, but I can't answer that. It's not my story to tell."

Gabe was proud of Kara for keeping Joni's secret, but he was also pissed off. He wanted to know everything about the little blonde. Kara had become much more confident under Nixon's and Nate's loving care and even though he wanted to continue to grill her, he just nodded his head.

"Okay, little sub. What *can* you tell me about her?"

Kara took a sip of her drink and tilted her head slightly. When Nixon shifted behind her, pulled her back against his body, and wrapped his arms around her, she relaxed against her Dom and sighed. "What do you want to know?"

"Everything," Nic answered in a firm voice.

"I don't feel comfortable talking about someone who isn't here."

"How about you answer a few questions then?" Tom suggested.

Kara nodded. "I can do that, but only ones I think are appropriate."

"What does she do for a living?" Gabe asked.

"She works in a restaurant as a bar manager, but if you ask me, she manages the whole place. When she has any spare time she also likes to write."

"What does she write?" Nic questioned.

Kara looked away before meeting Nic's eyes. "Romance."

"There's more to that answer isn't there, Kara?" Tom speculated.

Kara nodded again. "If you want an in-depth answer, you'll have to ask Joni."

"Fair enough," Tom said. "Does she live locally?"

"Yes."

"Which side of town?" Nic sipped from his beer.

"Not far from where I used to live."

"So she's struggling?" Gabe more stated than asked.

"Joni has been struggling by choice. She is saving up for her own restaurant, but I think she should be concentrating on her writing. She has such a talent for it."

"Where does she work?" Nic queried.

"Why isn't she concentrating on her writing?" Tom enquired.

"Uh…"

Gabe noted the expressions flitting across Kara's face and knew she didn't want to answer so decided to put her out of her misery and asked the next question rolling around in his mind. "How old is she?"

"How old do you think she is?" Kara asked.

"Twenty-two," Tom guessed.

"No."

"Twenty-one?" Nic frowned.

"No."

"Twenty-five." Gabe gave a stab in the dark. Joni had a young fresh face and it was hard to gauge her age, but from the sadness and wariness he'd seen in her eyes, she was older than her physical years.

"Yes."

"Thank God," Tom muttered loud enough for Gabe and Nic to hear.

They were all over thirty and didn't want to rob the cradle. As they'd matured they'd vowed never to play with anyone under the age of twenty-two. Gabe had just turned thirty-four but it didn't bother him that he was nine years older than Joni. In his opinion, age didn't matter in the course of love and attraction, but some people had weird values about men dating younger women or vice versa. Not that he cared what anyone else thought about him and his friends, but he was getting older and wanted to have a permanent relationship.

He sighed with frustration and ran his fingers through his hair. Joni was gorgeous and sexy. He wished she was still here so he and his buddies could get to know her, but from the way she'd rushed off, she wasn't the least bit interested in getting to know them.

That didn't mean she wasn't attracted to them, though. He'd seen the way her nipples had been pushing against the blue material of her shirt and the way her breathing had escalated as she looked up at them. Plus, there was the way she'd shivered when she shook hands with each of them.

He wanted to ask Kara for Joni's address so he could go and visit, but knew she wouldn't be comfortable giving out personal information about her friend. He admired her for that, but he didn't know how he was going to learn more about Joni any other way.

"Does Joni have a boyfriend?" Nic asked.

"No."

Gabe nearly sagged with relief when he heard Kara answer but then tensed up when Tom asked his question.

"Is she into women?"

"No." Kara stepped to the side and then clutched at Nixon's and Nate's hands. "Guys, I really don't think she wants a man or men right now. She's concentrating on her career."

"Has she had anything published?" Gabe asked.

"Yes, but it takes time for an author to see any earnings. Plus, there's the fact with all the people stealing and sharing books online. When she told me about that it made me so angry. Here she is working so hard to get her career off the ground only to have others stealing her work. That's like someone breaking into my home and taking money from my purse or getting into my wages and taking it.

"How can other people live with their consciences knowing they are stealing? I'd bet my ass they'd be screaming the house down if someone took money from their pay or purse, or went into their home and stole their belongings."

"Some people have no morals, that's for sure," Nic said with an indignant look on his face.

Gabe was sure he probably looked just as angry as Nic and Tom did. He hated that some people had no sense of right or wrong and didn't think stealing was wrong. He wished he could do something to help Joni out, but he couldn't, especially when she didn't seem interested in him and his pals. He just hoped that one day real soon he and his friends would meet the woman of their dreams.

He wanted to be able to hold his woman through the night and wake up to her each morning. He wanted to make a life and have kids. None of the subs in the club did anything for him anymore. Of course, when they'd first joined Gabe, Nic, and Tom had played every weekend but it got old real soon, until all he ever came to the club for was to socialize. He didn't want to have meaningless sex with a woman. He wanted to love and be loved in return.

Sex for the sake of sex just didn't do it for him anymore.

They said good-bye to Kara, Nixon, and Nate and headed out.

Just as he reached to door handle to the front passenger seat of Nic's truck, all three of their cell phones went off. Gabe drew his phone from his pocket and glanced at the text message.

"Fuck!" He looked over at Tom to see him standing next to his open truck door.

"What the hell?" Tom spat. "That's two waitresses in two months."

"Something has to be wrong," Nic said. "We've never had anyone leave in quick succession before."

"You're right," Gabe said, rubbing a hand over his face. "I think we need to spend some time at the pub and find out what the hell is going on."

"Yeah," Tom agreed. "We're going to have to advertise for another waitress."

"Toby's usually real good at handling staff issues," Nic said. "We need to call a meeting lunchtime tomorrow and this time I think we should do the hiring."

"Toby will get his nose out of joint. He's been hiring and firing for years." Gabe leaned on the truck.

"That may be, but something is going ass up." Tom moved a couple of steps closer.

"I'll put an ad online tomorrow morning, but I doubt we'll get anyone to interview by lunch." Gabe kept his eyes on his cell as he texted the pub manager, Toby, to set up a meeting and was pleased when he got an almost instant reply. "Okay, we have a meeting at 1 p.m."

"Do you think Toby's losing it?" Nic asked.

"He was fine the last time we saw him." Gabe shoved his cell back in his pocket.

"Yeah, but he's getting on. He could have a touch of Alzheimer's or something."

"Shit. I hadn't thought of that."

"Surely our people wouldn't quit just because Toby's sick." Tom sighed.

"Won't know until we have our meeting. Let's not cross any bridges until we get to them."

"Okay," Tom replied. "See you at home."

Gabe and Nic got into the truck. Gabe hoped Toby was okay, but he had a horrible feeling they were going to need to spend more time at the pub. Not that he minded. He actually enjoyed the pub they owned. They were doing so well he'd been thinking of expanding and buying another hotel.

Tom enjoyed doing security and although he and Nic had started out in security, too, he and Nic preferred to be outdoors doing gardening than being inside all the time. They had started up a landscaping business and spent most of their time planning and setting up gardens for people who didn't have the time to do such things themselves.

And as those thoughts flittered through his mind, he began to wonder if buying and doing up another pub was viable when none of them had been spending anytime at the one they already owned. He would need to talk to his friends and ask their opinion, but for right now he couldn't keep his thoughts from wandering back to Joni.

"Do you think she wasn't interested?" Nic glanced at him before turning his eyes back to the road.

"Did you study her body language?" Gabe countered.

"Yeah. She was attracted to us, but she didn't like it." Nic sighed.

"She was scared."

"Yeah, but why?"

"That's the million dollar question, isn't it?"

"I admire Kara for sticking to her guns and staying tight lipped about her friend, but it was hard not to push her for more."

"Agreed. That little lady has come a long way under her Doms' care."

"If we had the chance, we'd be able to get to the heart of Joni's fears, too."

"You and I know that, but I can't see her letting us get near her." Gabe shifted in his seat to look at Nic. "We don't even know where she lives."

"Damn. I had a good feeling about her." Nic slowed the truck, flicked the indicator on, and turned into the driveway.

"I did, too."

"Fuck!" Nic shut off the engine. "I don't think we'll ever see her again."

"Don't say that," Gabe said before getting out of the truck. "You never know what's around the corner."

* * * *

Joni walked into her boss's office and took a seat when he waved his hand toward the chair. She had no idea what was going on or if she'd done something wrong but she guessed she was about to find out.

"Joni, you're an efficient worker and the customers all love you, but I'm sorry to say I have to let you go." Gerrard Wattle leaned back in his chair, the pen in his hand rolling over his fingers as if he were nervous.

"What?" Joni gasped, a knot of dread forming in her stomach.

She'd just worked her ass off for the lunch crowd at Gerrard's Restaurant and now that the rush was over he was firing her?

What the hell?

"Why?"

"My nephew has just finished a hospitality course and needs work. I really hate to do this but family does come first."

Joni stared at him with stupefaction. She had worked at this restaurant for the last five years, taking all the overtime she could, filling in for sick staff and he was rewarding her by releasing her? Because of nepotism?

"Gerrard—" Joni didn't get to say anymore because he cut her off.

"I want to thank you for the years you've worked here, Joni. I know if it wasn't for you there would have been times where we may have had to close the doors. I have written you a sterling reference and have put a little extra in your severance pay." Gerrard rose to his feet, gripped her elbow, helping her from the chair, and guided her to the door. He literally nudged her through the opening, stuffed a large envelope into her hands, and closed the door.

Joni blinked as tears welled in her eyes. She'd helped Gerrard set up his damn restaurant, and although she mainly tended bar, if it wasn't for her, the place never would have gotten off the ground. She was the one who interviewed and hired the staff, including the apprentice chef who now had a great reputation. And this was how he repaid her?

Fucking asshole!

She'd done way more than bar work. In fact, she'd been more of a manager than Gerrard.

She'd known something was going on because every time she saw Gerrard he only met her eyes briefly and he'd never done that before. For the last few weeks he'd been acting out of the ordinary and now she knew why.

Her chest was aching with disappointment and frustration and even though she wanted to go back into Gerrard's office, she wasn't about to make a fool of herself and beg for her job back. Not that it would do any good anyway.

She'd met Gerrard's stuck-up sister, Antoinette. That woman reminded her of a shark. When she had her teeth in something she wasn't going to let go.

Joni stared about the restaurant and was glad the staff had already finished with the lunchtime cleanup. She'd already restocked the bar fridges and wiped down the bar. She knew she should go into the kitchens and say good-bye to everyone, but she knew if she did she wouldn't be able to keep it together.

She drew herself out of the shock and hurried toward the bar, grabbed her purse, and left without a backward glance. It didn't matter that her work colleagues had been friendly to her and she them. She'd never socialized with any of them outside of work and wondered if they would even realize she was missing. Joni doubted it very much. Gerrard's Restaurant staff knew their jobs back to front and worked well individually as well as collectively, as an intrinsic part of a well-oiled machine. Gerrard obviously had no trouble replacing those parts.

Joni entered her one-bedroom efficiency, dumped her purse and the large envelope on her small dining table, and headed for her bedroom. She stripped out of her black skirt, white shirt and, after turning the shower on, got in.

The warm water rushed over her head and body, easing some of the tension in her muscles, but it didn't take the pain in her neck or head away. She washed her hair and body and then just stood there with her eyes closed as she tried to come to terms with being unemployed.

A sob escaped her mouth and the first tears ran down her face mixing with the water flowing over her. She tried to push her pain back but it wouldn't be denied. She cried until she had nothing left, feeling drained and weary, and finally turned the water off.

After drying off and dressing in her worn, comfortable jeans and a T-shirt she went to the kitchen and put the kettle on. She stared at the envelope and with a fit of pique tore it open and tipped out the contents.

Gerrard had been true to his word and given her a great reference and when she saw the check she picked it up. She snorted with disbelief at the "bonus" Gerrard had given her. For five years of hard work he'd given her an extra five hundred dollars.

Joni snorted and then started laughing. She laughed with incredulousness until the tears flowed again. After a moment, the anger came back and she held onto it. She wasn't going to cry about losing her job. What she needed to do was find another right away. She didn't care that she would probably have to work her way back up in the ranks. She was going do the best she could and one day, hopefully in the not too distant future she would be able to snob Gerrard and his bitch of a sister.

She was the reason his restaurant had survived and grown and she would find her way to the top again. Maybe one day she would be able to buy her own place and steal all his customers.

What she really wanted to do was concentrate on her writing. She'd written a few erotic romance books but the royalties weren't enough for her to survive on. And although the writing bug was still there, a deep yearning in her gut, she needed to work to survive.

Her plans were to buy a restaurant of her own and instill loyal staff to run the place, so she could write whenever she wanted. She knew she'd have to spend a lot of time finding the right people to hire so she could achieve her dreams, and also that she would need to spend a couple of years earning a good reputation for her own restaurant or bar, but those dreams seemed to be getting further and further out of reach.

Joni wondered if she would ever attain any of the goals she'd set herself and became a bit despondent, because she couldn't see anything she wanted to happen, happening anytime soon.

Chapter Three

Joni had been searching jobs online for the last few hours but so far hadn't found anything appropriate. Of course, there were plenty of cleaning jobs and such, and although there was definitely nothing wrong with those jobs, she didn't want to have to take just anything quite yet.

With the money she'd been paid for vacation and the measly bonus Gerrard had given her, she figured she'd have a couple of weeks to keep looking until she found a job she wanted to do. She had some savings she'd put away over the years but she had no intention of touching that unless she was absolutely desperate. That nest egg was to be used to buy her own place or maybe even go into partnership with someone. It was her dream to be her own boss and not have to answer to anyone ever again, but now she could see that going out the door.

She was about to give up for the day because her neck and head were giving her hell and the tension was seeping into her shoulders, too, but decided to peruse one more page.

When she saw the heading of the first advert at the top of her page she nearly jumped out of her seat to do a jig, but she took a deep breath, pushed her nervous excitement down, and began to read.

Hotel Bar Manager.

Immediate start for the right person.

Must have at least three years hospitality experience in a high volume bar environment.

Tick.

Must have at least two years beverage and wine service experience as well as a working knowledge of all beverage products, menu items and equipment used to perform these duties.

Tick.

Working knowledge of kitchen operations and health and safety regulations is a must. As well as a professional appearance and demeanor.

Tick.

If you have the above requirements please e-mail your CV and cover letter to the supplied e-mail address.

Joni's belly fluttered with nervousness, but she was determined to send her resume as soon as possible. When she glanced at the clock on her laptop she saw it was already after five o'clock. She found her CV file, checked it over, added a few updates, and then scanned the reference Gerrard had given her. By the time she'd written her cover letter and attached the files it was 5:15. Her finger hovered over the send button and as she pressed it she closed her eyes and drew a deep breath. When she opened her eyes again she saw the message on the screen advising her she had been successful in sending her e-mail.

Now all she had to do was wait.

She knew it could take at least a couple of weeks before she heard anything if she was actually shortlisted and got to the interview stage, and although she knew she should set up e-mail alerts for jobs she was interested in, she was too tired.

All she wanted to do now was grab something to eat, curl up on her small sofa, and read or watch TV before going to bed.

Tomorrow was soon enough to look for more jobs.

Joni went to the kitchen and made herself a sandwich and a cup of tea. Just as she finished eating she heard her computer ding alerting her to an incoming e-mail. She wanted to rush over and see who it was from, but trepidation had her belly fluttering with nerves, so she took the time to wash her dishes first.

When she was done, she drew a deep breath and walked slowly back to the small two-seater sofa and coffee table. She really didn't want to look because she had a feeling it was a reply to her job application and if it was, she didn't think it would be good news. No one ever responded so quickly to applicants.

She sat down, moving the curser on top of the e-mail which was indeed a response from whoever was dealing with perusing CVs and interviews. Her heart stuttered and she tried to remember if the job had been listed by an employment agency or by the actual hotel owner itself, but she was so nervous she couldn't get her brain to function or remember.

"Well, nothing for it, girl. You may as well find out one way or the other," she muttered to herself and clicked open.

When she saw she had an interview the very next day she jumped to her feet, screamed with joy, and pumped a fist into the air. "Yes. Yes. Yes. Stick that up your ass Gerard."

* * * *

Nic was about to climb the front porch steps to go inside, but something was niggling at him about another waitress leaving. Toby was always so organized, but it seemed things were starting to fall apart. He knew he wouldn't be able to sleep if he didn't find out what was going on. He and Gabe had worked their asses off today, tidying up an acre lot which looked like it hadn't been tended to for years.

The only break he and Gabe had was a half hour at lunch when they met with Toby. Even though Toby seemed fine there were a couple of times when the older man seemed to just stare off into space and didn't respond to either of them.

That didn't bode well with him and he'd ordered Toby to go to the doctors to get checked out. He hoped the older man wasn't ill, but if he was, hopefully he'd sought medical treatment early enough.

His body ached from the constant lifting and carrying of tree limbs, discarded loads of bricks and such, but it was a good ache. He loved working outdoors and although he sometimes finished the day exhausted and sore he was proud of what he and Gabe had accomplished in such a short amount of time.

"I think we should go and see if Toby is all right." Nic turned to face Gabe.

Gabe paused with his foot on the step and the other on the pathway and then he sighed. "Yeah, you're right." He glanced at his watch. "I thought we would have heard back from him by now."

"Me, too."

"You can drive." Nic tossed the keys over to him as he began to walk back to the truck. "I'll call Tom and see if he can meet us."

"He was doing DM at the club this afternoon wasn't he?" Gabe asked after he started the engine.

"Yeah and then he was supposed to watch the security monitors tonight, but I'm sure Turner can get someone to cover him." Nic unlocked his cell with the swipe of a finger and then he pressed speed dial. When he'd finished the call he glanced at Gabe. "Tom will meet us at the hotel as soon as he can."

Gabe nodded in acknowledgement. Moments later he parked the truck out back of the hotel.

Nic glanced around the dim interior searching for Toby. He and Gabe had come in through the back door and since the office door was wide open he saw Toby wasn't sitting behind his desk as usual. They stopped in at the kitchen and saw their harried chef barking out orders to the apprentices and kitchen hands, but Nic noticed there seemed to be a couple of people missing.

Brent Prichard, their chef, glanced up and the stress on his face eased when he saw them. "Thank God you're here."

Nic and Gabe moved closer so they wouldn't have to yell over the clattering of pots and pans.

"What's up?" Gabe asked.

"Toby's been sent to the hospital."

"Shit! Is he okay? Why the hell didn't he call one of us?"

"His doctor actually called the phone here. Toby apparently has epilepsy and has had a mild stroke."

"Fuck! I knew there was something wrong when we saw him at lunch. I should have asked if he wanted me to drive him to his doctor's."

"Why didn't you contact us?" Gabe asked.

Brent snorted. "I haven't had the time. I've been too busy trying to keep everything running smoothly. Plus, the call only came in about fifteen minutes ago."

"You're short a few hands. Where are they?" Nic asked.

"Out trying to serve at the bar."

"Damn. Okay, thanks Brent. We owe you one." Gabe nodded his head.

"If there's anything we can do just give a yell," Nic said before following Gabe toward the doorway.

"Just send my kitchen hands back," Brent yelled.

Nic lifted his hand in acknowledgement and hurried to the bar. He and Gabe served drink after drink and he sighed when there was a lull and decided to check the office. "I'm just going to check the paperwork. Call if it gets busy again."

Gabe nodded but kept filling the order he was working on.

As Nic walked down the hallway, Tom entered the back door and after he quickly explained what was going on, Tom hurried out to help Gabe.

Nic sat at the desk and started checking e-mails. When he saw there were a couple of hundred in the inbox he wondered if Tom had managed to put an advert online for a new bartender. He, Gabe, and Tom had compiled the ad yesterday but he hadn't known his friend had already posted it.

When he began reading he realized Toby must have known he was sick because the job applications were for a Hotel Bar Manager.

Their manager must have signed in and changed the position being advertised yesterday afternoon. He felt bad that they hadn't known about Toby's illness, but he and his friends would do everything they could to make sure he was treated by the best doctors, and they would pay for all his medical expenses. Toby was a loyal hard worker and deserved their help.

Nic vaguely acknowledged Brent when he brought him some dinner as he continued to read through e-mail after e-mail. He was at number fifty and skimmed over the cover letter to the name at the bottom. His heart flipped in his chest when he saw Joni Meeks and he drew in a deep breath. His wiped his sweaty palms on his jeans and then he opened the attachments.

The more he read of Joni's CV, the more excited he became. She had all the qualifications needed to run the hotel and he immediately sent a reply setting up an interview for the next day and didn't bother looking at anymore applicants. If he had his way Joni would be working for them ASAP.

After making sure the BOM, bill of materials, was filled out and saved, he grabbed his empty plate, dropped it off in the kitchen with a thanks to Brent, and was about to hurry out to the bar but stopped to question the chef.

"Brent, did you know Toby was ill?"

Brent frowned and shook his head. "Nah, he was acting kind of weird, but not once did I stop and think he was sick. He wasn't pale and even though he's had a mild stroke none of it showed with his motor skills."

"What do you mean by weird? And do you have any idea why the last two bar attendants quit?"

"I caught Toby staring off into space a couple of times and I asked him if he was okay, but he didn't respond. Then he would blink and look around before he went back to whatever he was doing. Those episodes never lasted more than thirty seconds and I'm sorry to say I put it down to him having things on his mind. If I'd known he was sick I would have called an ambulance and you guys straight away. "

"Don't blame yourself, Brent. I think Toby was in denial and if he wasn't about to seek help and he didn't confess to the illness, there was nothing any of us could do."

"Yeah, I suppose you're right. It's just I feel a little guilty, is all."

"We do, too, but at least we got him to see a doctor before it was too late." Nic sighed and ran his fingers through his hair. "What happened with the bar attendants?"

"That had nothing to do with Toby," Brent said. "One of the women was only filling in until she got married. Toby knew that and had already interviewed someone to fill in for her, but there were so few applicants he had to take what there was. Well, that turned out to be a mistake. The asshole he hired was drinking the merchandise while he was working. When Toby caught him he fired him on the spot."

"What about our casuals? There aren't any here."

Brent shook his head. "Most of them were college students and they were great workers, but the school year finished a couple of weeks ago and most of them were graduates and have moved on to pursue their careers."

"Damn! Do we have any casuals left?"

"Yeah. Judy, the single mom, still works here, but when I found her number and called to see if she could work, she told me her daughter was sick and she was taking her to the emergency room."

"Have you heard from her? Is her little one okay?"

"Yeah, she'll be fine. Apparently she's scheduled to get her tonsils out tomorrow morning."

"So Judy won't be coming to work for at least a week," Nic said to himself more than Brent.

"She's asked for two weeks and I couldn't very well say no."

"You did the right thing."

"So what are we going to do?" Brent asked. "I can't work in the kitchens and the bar, plus I need my people to feed everyone coming in for meals."

"We had an advert online for a manager and after going through some of the applicants, I think I found the perfect candidate. I've set up an interview for tomorrow. If this person works out and can start right away, they can start hiring some more people and take care of things.

"We're also going to be working the bar at night until we have more staff."

"Okay. I hope this person works out for you."

"Me, too, and thanks for looking after things tonight. You all will be getting a bonus in your pay for going above and beyond your job descriptions."

The kitchen staff cheered and Brent stepped forward to shake Nic's hand and then he hurried out to the bar.

When he saw that the place was nearly empty he glanced at his watch and noticed it was nearly eleven o'clock. He hadn't realized how much time had passed. Gabe and Tom were wiping down the bar and putting the clean glasses from the dishwasher back up in the racks.

"Everything okay?" Tom asked as he emptied out the slosh bucket into the sink.

"Yes. In fact, things couldn't be better, besides Toby, of course." Nic sat on a barstool and took a swig from the beer bottle Gabe passed him.

"What's going on?" Gabe asked.

"I think Toby must have known he was sick because when I checked the e-mails there were a couple of hundred applicants for a hotel bar manager."

"He changed the ad? Shit! I feel really bad for not spending more time here and talking to Toby. If we had, we could have gotten him medical treatment faster." Tom placed both his hands on the bar and leaned forward.

"Tom, you have vacation time up your sleeve at the club, don't you?" Nic asked.

"Yeah. Why?"

"I want you to call Turner and ask for time off."

"Okay? Why?"

"Because we need to work here until we have more staff."

"How the hell are we going to do that?" Gabe bit out. "We have our landscaping business and sometimes we start before dawn. If we burn the candles at both ends we're going to end up burned out."

"It'll only be for a couple of weeks, Gabe. If we talk to our clients I'm sure they'll understand if we start a bit later.

"Plus, I think you are both going to want to be here."

"Why?" Gabe snapped.

"There was an applicant I think you'll both agree to want to hire on the spot."

"Who?" Tom raised an eyebrow.

"Joni Meeks."

Tom exhaled long and loudly and the tension eased from Gabe's face and body.

"Are you shitting me?" Gabe asked skeptically.

"Would I joke about something like that?" Nic was the one raising his eyebrow this time.

"Have you set up an interview?" Tom asked as he moved around the bar and began putting the stools up on the gleaming wood surface.

Nic stood up and helped him.

"Yes. Tomorrow at ten."

Tom pulled his cell out of his pocket and dialed. "Hi, Turner, sorry to call so late, but I'm going to need to take some vacation time." He paused while he listened to the club owner's response.

"Yes, I know its short notice but our bar manager is sick and we don't think he'll be coming back. We need to work here until we can get more staff in." Tom paused again. "What about Sonny?

"Okay. Thanks heaps, Turner. I'll let you know as soon as I'm available. Take care." Tom disconnected the call. "I'm in."

"We're supposed to start landscaping the Simpson's yard tomorrow," Gabe said.

"Yes, but we are actually ahead of schedule already. We thought we wouldn't have that yard ready to start landscaping until the day after tomorrow. We've cleared everything out and just need to draw up the plans and then we can start on the garden beds and the planting. I'm sure Mrs. Simpson wouldn't mind if we call and explain first thing," Nic said.

"Okay. You're right, but you can call her. If she's going to be pissed off, you can take the flack."

"Done." Nic smiled and rubbed his hands together. He had a good feeling about this, but after the way Joni had scurried away last night, he wasn't sure she would take the job. And that made him wonder why she was even looking.

He'd heard her talking to Kara at the club about how much she loved working at the restaurant, but that was a question he would have to ask her tomorrow. He was so excited, he knew he was going to have trouble sleeping and, from the gleam in his friends' eyes, they were just as exuberant as he was.

Chapter Four

Joni was so nervous her palms were damp. She sat outside the Three Comrades Hotel and tried to calm her breathing. She was fifteen minutes early and although she wanted to go inside and get her interview over with, she wasn't sure anyone was here, yet. The doors were closed and although the hotel wouldn't open for another hour, she would have thought someone would be here by now.

Maybe they were keeping the doors closed in case people tried to walk in before opening. When she realized what she was doing, she took a few more deep breaths and exhaled slowly, pushing all thoughts from her mind. She grabbed her purse, CV, and accreditation certificates as well as the reference Gerrard had given her and got out of her car. With her held high and her shoulders back, she dug down for the confidence she had with her work and walked toward the door. She didn't bother knocking but gripped the handle and opened the door. It opened so easily she had to take two small side steps so she wouldn't fall on her ass and then she entered.

The interior was dim after the bright spring sunshine and she had to blink a few times to accustom her sight to the darkness. When she saw three men sitting at the bar she headed over to them. As she got closer, her steps faltered when she saw who it was. Heat filled her cheeks as she slowed her walk and stopped a few feet from the men she'd met at the BDSM club.

Tom got to his feet and smiled as he held his hand out to her. "Hello, Joni. It's good to see you again."

Joni cleared her throat as she clasped his proffered hand and hoped her face wasn't as red as it felt. "Hi, Tom." She quickly withdrew her hand and hoped the shiver working up her spine wasn't noticeable as she tried not to shudder.

"Joni, you look lovely." Gabe eyed her body up and down as he grasped her hands.

She mentally cursed when she felt her breasts swell and her nipples bead into tight little buds. "Thank you."

"Hey, beautiful." Nic nudged Gabe aside and was holding her hand but he didn't shake it like she expected. She nearly sighed when his thumb caressed over the skin on then she quickly tugged it away from him.

"Have a seat, Joni." Tom drew her gaze and patted the seat of the stool he'd pulled out for her.

She sat down and when she realized she was panting she drew another deep breath, holding it for a moment before releasing it.

How can these three handsome men affect me? Why do they arouse me? I've seen other men just as good and never reacted this way with them. Why these men and why

"So." Gabe's voice was so close and she swore his breath brush against her ear, but when she turned her head his gaze he wasn't as close to her as she thought.

For God's sake, get it together, Joni.

"Tell us a little about yourself."

Joni told them how she'd worked from the age of ten as a kitchen hand at a small, local restaurant and after high school how she'd gotten her hospitality degree online schooling. She told them how she'd hired staff, ordered stock, and done the bill of materials on the computer.

"From the sound of it you pretty much ran that rest," Nic said.

"Um..." Joni hesitated and nervously licked her lips. She didn't want to sound too big-headed, but as she thought about it she realized it was true. She had run Gerrard's Restaurant and made it what it was today. "I suppose you could say that."

"So why do y leave?" Tom frowned.

"I don't. I di really hated telling them that she was fired because she di them to think she was incompetent, but guessed the tru me out if they called Gerrard to check up on her. "I was f "

"What the h

Gabe soun and Joni's first instinct was to get off the stool and move n him. When he raised his hand she flinched. He gave her a ook but then ran his hand over his face. "Are you scared of i

Joni shook no, but she could see skepticism in his eyes. She lowered h the bar and then met his eyes again.

"I would urt you or any other woman," Gabe said emphatically uch sincerity, she believed him unequivocally.

"Has som you, Joni?" Nic asked.

She glan m before looking away and shook her head. Although she wasn't about to tell these three manly men her life history. here for an interview. Nothing more, nothing less. She qui ged the subject. "I was let go because my boss, Gerrard, dec ire his nephew."

"At leas you a great reference."

"You lo ?"

"Yes."

"I have t," Tom said. "Have you got it with you?'

Joni pa r her CV and reference to him.

"When start?" Nic asked.

She w ed because it sounded like he and his friends were going to h n the spot and they hadn't even called Gerrard yet.

"Um, r you want me to."

"This ng, love," Tom said as he glanced up from her CV. "Your las an idiot."

Joni s nd felt all her tension drain away. It was nice to hear someone n't really know giving her praise and she liked it, a lot. She sat a little straighter, her confidence lity to do a good job causing her to think that just maybe neant to be. She would have to be vigilant though and try ar attraction under wraps and hidden from them. It would be arrassing if her prospective employers worked out that she h for them. She glanced at Gabe and Nic and saw they w udying her intently and had a feeling she hadn't hidden any them. She knew it was ludicrous, but she felt like all three men could see right through her walls, straight into her heart

"Thank you," Joni finally remembered to answ

"You're welcome, love," Tom said. "W let our employees know when we're happy with them n they go beyond expectations we give extra incentives an by paying out bonuses."

"Wow, that's so nice."

"That reminds me," Nic said. "I've given Brent e kitchen staff a bonus this week for keeping things together l?

"Good." Gabe nodded. "Joni, will you come i ffice and help me compile an advert for more bartenders?"

"Okay."

* * * *

Gabe took hold of Joni's elbow and helped her tool. He would have kept holding her if she hadn't moved asid oked up at him as if she were waiting for him to lead the way looked down at her, he realized how petite she was.

She couldn't have been more than five foot three but she had a gloriously feminine body on her with all the ri es. Her blonde hair was up in some sort of knot at the back of l with a few loose tendrils dangling beside her face which n r look damn sexy. Her white blouse only had the first button and he wondered if she had a poor body image, which was utte culous as far as he was because she was absolutely perfect in his eyes. He would ...ng he could to boost her confidence if that were the case, b...for later.

He swept hi...in front of him, urging her to go first. The first step she to...tative but she kept going as he directed her verbally. He co...the way her shoulders were stiff and her hands weren't ...er sides that she was uncomfortable being in the lead and tha...hope. Hope that she was indeed submissive in all aspects o...than her job. He'd heard how passionate she was about her ...wondered why she hadn't started up her own place, but gue...because of financial times being so hard, she didn't have the...do it.

Maybe if ...rked out with her and them in a relationship they could bri...as a partner. But again that was for the future. He couldn't h...atch the sway of her slim hips and sexy ass. It was all he co...t to move closer and run his hands over those soft, yet musc...ks.

"Wait!" ...ed for her to turn and was pleased when she did immediately. ...to introduce you to the chef and kitchen staff." He pointed t...r on his right and again waited for her to precede him.

When h...d behind her all eyes turned to look at Joni curiously be...ng to him.

"Brent, ...ou to meet our new hotel manager." Gabe placed a hand on ...ower back, urging her closer to the chef. "Joni Meeks, mee...Prichard."

Brent w...s hand on a towel and then held it out in greeting. "I am so pl...meet you, Joni. Now I can concentrate on running the kitchen...

Joni to...t's hand and smiled. "Nice to meet you, too. If you have any ...s at all please don't hesitate to come to me." Joni drew her ...m Brent's and looked at the other employees. "Any of you. Th...at I'm here for."

Brent introduced the rest of the staff and then Gabe guided her out. They entered the office and he indicated that she sit on the chair behind the desk. He grabbed one from near the wall and carried it over next to her before sitting down.

"Okay, get yourself familiar with the software programs and if you have any questions, ask." Gabe remained silent while she did just that. She moved through the different screens quickly and efficiently obviously already acquainted with it all.

"I don't have any problems with this. I'm glad to see everything's up to date, though. That will make my transition a lot easier, not having to catch up on things."

"Good." Gabe reached for a pad and pen that was on the desk and made sure to brush against her arm as he did so. He had to bite the inside of his cheek when he saw her shiver from the corner of his eye. He was glad that she was attracted to him and, if he was right, she wasn't impervious to Tom or Nic either. When they met the other night at the club they had all watched her intently and seen the signs of interest from her body. Her mind had definitely not been on board, though. He hoped that he and his friends could change it for her.

Gabe had heard some of her conversation with Kara and knew she'd been hurt. He wanted to ask her who had hurt her and what had been done to her, but knew she didn't trust him or his friends as yet. It was going to take time to build a rapport with her and gain conviction from her, and maybe then she would be willing to open up and talk to them.

Over the next hour they mapped out an advert for casual bar and wait staff and he gave her the passwords to access their job site account. She was fast and efficient and, before he knew it, she'd posted the ad.

"Do you have anything else you'd like to show me?" Joni asked.

"Not right now. Nic and I wouldn't normally be here as we own a landscaping and gardening business. Tom helps out now and then when we're bogged down, but he's normally working nights at the Club of Dominance with security."

He watched as she licked her lips nervously and when she frowned he could tell she had questions. He stayed silent without prompting her and hoped she would ask whatever was rolling around in her head.

"Why do you like hurting women?"

Gabe tensed up and when he caught movement from the corner of his eye he glanced up and saw that Nic and Tom were standing in the doorway. He quickly averted his eyes back to Joni's and hoped she didn't see his friends. He didn't want her to be uncomfortable, but then he thought that it would be better if she knew they were listening. He didn't want to hide anything from her because she might feel as if they were untrustworthy and deceptive, and that was no way to gain her confidence.

"Come in, guys."

Joni turned to look Tom's and Nic's way before lowering her eyes as her face tinged pink.

Gabe clasped her chin between his finger and thumb, turning her face back toward his and he watched with satisfaction as her pupils reacted by contracting before dilating.

"We don't like hurting women or children in any way, shape or form."

"But—"

"Just listen to us explain before you ask your questions. Okay?" Gabe was pleased when she pressed her lips together and nodded. He released his hold on her and nearly sighed with disappointment when she scooted her chair farther away from him.

"Don't ever be scared of me, Tom, or Nic."

"I'm not."

Gabe studied her body language and was glad that she was being sincere.

"BDSM is not abuse," Tom started.

"Far from it," Nic reiterated.

"Have you ever been tired of making decisions? Of wanting to just hand everything on your plate over to someone else to deal with?" Gabe asked.

Joni gave a slight nod of her head.

"BDSM is freeing to those who want and need to give up control." Tom moved to the sofa near the far wall and sat down. Nic followed and sat beside him.

Gabe never removed his eyes from Joni and noticed the way her eyes perused their bodies up and down. He glanced down at her chest when her arms twitched and saw that her nipples were hard little points pressing against her shirt. When she shifted in her seat and crossed her legs and she squeezed her thighs together, he had to bite back a grin.

She was affected by all of them and that gave him hope.

"Small amounts of pain cause endorphins to race through a person's system and heightens pleasure," Gabe said in a calm modulated voice.

"But what if the person's not into pain?"

"Most people aren't." Nic leaned forward and rested his elbows on his thighs, dangling his hands between his legs. "There are a few who are into masochism but the Club of Dominance doesn't condone any hard pain. The members and staff have to read the policies and sign to agree to those rules. First and foremost a sub's well-being is to be protected. Everyone involved in a scene knows that the motto 'safe, sane and consensual are to be adhered to at all times."

"Anyone breaking the rules would be thrown out and never allowed back. There are safe words in place that can and will stop play," Tom explained. "If the sub on the receiving end of the play is unsure they can use the word 'yellow' which will stop a scene temporarily so the Dom, or Doms, and sub can discuss the situation and get to the uncertainty or fear their submissive is experiencing."

"Trust is a huge component in BDSM play," Gabe said. "It's the Dom's job to make sure he reads his sub's body language. To know that they aren't taking her beyond her limits."

"And if they do?" Joni asked.

"Then the sub uses the word 'red and everything stops." Gabe could see her mind going over what they'd told her. He wondered if she had an inkling that she was submissive. He doubted it very much. Unless a sub had experienced BDSM or read about it, the sub would never even suspect their deferential tendencies.

Joni's surname was more appropriate than she would suspect. She was meek in every way except her career, which was good for him and his friends. They didn't want a slave or an obsequious person twenty-four seven. He and his buddies wanted a woman who would submit to them in the bedroom, but stand up and be counted in every other aspect of her life.

Joni wasn't a pushover, thank god. He had a feeling she had been holding herself back after she'd gotten hurt. He could practically feel the passion vibrating down deep inside of her and he wanted to be around if she ever let go and let her true self out. It was going to be a delicate operation dealing with her. They didn't want to break her, but set her free. But he suspected she was going to be a hard nut to crack. He hoped he was wrong, but after working security and having Dom training, plus the few relationships he'd had, he was damn good at reading people.

The relationships he'd had when he was younger hadn't lasted long and he knew that was mostly his fault. He'd always felt something was missing and after a few beers with Nic and Tom, he'd begun explaining how he felt. He wasn't surprised when they had admitted to feeling the same.

The day they'd met Turner Pike was the best day of their lives. Turner had called for a quote to landscape the garden at the club and after speaking to the man a few times he shocked them all by telling them they were dominants.

When Turner had told them about BDSM and suggested they attend the Dom classes, they had jumped in with both feet and never looked back. They had played with subs learning their craft and even shared a couple of times, but none of those women had engaged their hearts.

Joni was the first woman that held all their interest and he was determined to keep her in his life. Even if it was only as their bar manager. Hopefully in the not too distant future she would come to trust them and let them all explore the attraction they had for each other.

Only time would tell.

Chapter Five

Joni didn't want to be intrigued by what they were telling her, nor turned on, but she was. Never before had she responded to the mental images running through her mind. Then she realized it wasn't just their words that were making her horny. It was so much more than that.

These three men had such a commanding, confident presence she couldn't help be drawn to them. And that wasn't all. Yes, they were stunningly good-looking in a rugged, manly way, with their muscular physiques she'd never seen on anyone other than gym junkies before, but they weren't over the top in the overblown way some men were. They were well proportioned. They were all over six feet give or take a few inches and although they seemed quite relaxed as they tried to explain their sexual proclivities to her, she felt like they were coiled, ready to strike at any time and she was their prey.

There was an air of danger surrounding them, yet she knew they would never hurt her physically, which made her feel more secure than she ever had been in her life. But she wasn't about to let her guard down because the lessons she'd had from *the school of hard knocks* had shown her men couldn't be trusted.

She'd been totally devastated when her father had left her and her mother and although she'd missed him and blamed herself since she was a small child, figuring her recent bad behavior had something to do with him walking out, that had been nothing compared to when he'd come back after years of estrangement and killed her mom by running her over.

The pain of such betrayal had never left and neither had the anger that had turned to hatred. It didn't matter that the police had found a medical diagnosis from a doctor claiming her father was medically insane, nor that he had been charged and institutionalized never to be released. The grief and anger somehow never left her and she had been so vulnerable when she'd met John, aka Angus. He'd just proven to her that she was right in her regards to men. She'd vowed never to let another man into her life or her guard down again.

Her ex-boss hadn't helped in her opinion of the opposite sex. She felt like he'd used her for the last five years and when his business had gained the notoriety he'd been aiming for, thanks to her, she'd become superfluous.

The only thing that was a constant in her life was good old-fashioned hard work and self-reliability. Until someone proved her wrong she didn't think she'd be changing her opinion anytime soon.

Joni sighed when she realized she'd spaced out. When she glanced up at each of the men they were all looking at her with worried expressions on their faces, and she wondered if she'd given some of her thoughts away by her facial expressions. If she had there wasn't anything she could do about it now, but she wasn't about to voice any of her private thoughts.

"Okay," she said after thinking back over what she been last told. "The women who let men dominate them have an out if they want it. But what happens if the man or men don't take any notice?"

"That would never happen," Tom said. "There are security cameras everywhere which are monitored at all times the club is open. There are dungeon monitors who scout the place to make sure the subs and Doms play by the rules."

"Dungeon monitor?" Joni asked.

"Security guards, if you will," Gabe replied. "Dungeon monitors are usually experienced Doms. All Doms take a turn as monitors. Turner made sure that every qualified dominant member agreed to volunteer as a monitor."

"How can a person be qualified to be a Dom?"

"We attend classes," Nic answered.

"Why would you want to do that?" Joni asked.

"We like to be in control," Gabe began. "Being in control is a turn-on for a dominant just like giving up control is a turn-on for a submissive. Subs aren't the only ones who have their pleasures enhanced by endorphins. It's a rush when we can make a sub scream in ecstasy or send them deep into subspace."

"What's subspace?" Joni asked and hoped they hadn't heard the breathless quality of her voice. She couldn't believe all this talk was getting to her. Her pussy was so damn wet, her undies were uncomfortable, and her clit wouldn't stop its damn throbbing. It was like her heart had somehow connected to her pussy and every time it beat her clit ached and her cunt clenched, releasing more of her cream.

She'd never reacted this way in her life, not even with the sleazy, lying Angus, and didn't know what to make of it.

"Subspace is when the mind and body connect on a level so deep the sub goes into a dreamlike state. I heard Charlie say it was like floating on a cloud. Everything around her was pushed away yet she was highly aware of her Doms' movements at all times. She likened it to being in a state of hyperawareness yet floating surrealism." Gabe crossed his arms over his chest and waited for her response, because she was frowning again.

"That sounds like a total contradiction."

"I suppose it is," Tom said. "The only way a sub could ever know what subspace is like is if they experience it for themselves."

Joni narrowed her eyes at him and wondered if he was trying to challenge her into taking the bait he dangled. She may look like a dumb blonde but she wasn't that naïve. At least not anymore. "I'll take your word for it."

She decided it was time to get back to work and back onto things she knew about. "You're going to need to order more fresh vegetables, and since Brent has e-mailed through an extensive list of fresh herbs, and from the records I can see that's a regular occurrence, I think it would be better to set up planter boxes along the kitchen windows and grow them ourselves. That way he has whatever he needs on hand and can pick them as he needs them."

"That's a great idea," Tom said as he rose to his feet. "Do you want to handle that or should one of us?"

"I will."

Tom nodded, and then looked at his cell phone when it buzzed. "We need to get out to the bar, Nic. The regulars are starting to arrive."

Nic nodded and stood up. "I'm glad you applied for the job, Joni. I think you are going to be a valuable asset to us."

Joni's heart filled with warm fuzzies and she couldn't stop the smile that formed on her lips. "Thank you. I'll try not to let you all down."

Tom and Nic nodded and left the room.

"What time does the bar open and what are my working hours?" Joni asked.

"Brent and his team get here at ten to prep for lunch, although we only serve burgers and simple fare. Dinner is a little more opulent and our busiest time, but finger foods can be ordered, too. We don't like to have people drinking with no possibility of eating, too."

"That's smart. There is nothing worse than a drunk man with an empty stomach," Joni said.

* * * *

"I hope that's not from experience," Gabe said and could have cut out his tongue when she tensed up all over. He might have hit the proverbial nail on the head with that remark, but he suspected there was much more than that to her fears with men. He nearly sighed with relief when she started talking, but cringed inside when her voice came out in that cool, professional tone again. When they'd been explaining BDSM to her, she lost that cool collectiveness she tried to portray and he loved how her light voice had a hint of huskiness come through that he hadn't noticed before. He wished he could take his words back but he couldn't turn back the clock.

"Can I see the lunch and dinner menus?"

"Sure. They're out at the bar and bistro area." Gabe stood and was about to help Joni, but she was on her feet and striding toward the door before he could assist her. He ran his fingers through his hair in frustration and followed.

* * * *

Tom glanced up when Joni and Gabe sat at the bar. Gabe handed her the lunch and dinner menus but he could tell by the expression on his friend's face he was unhappy. Tom quirked an eyebrow at him but Gabe gave a slight shake of his head, and mouthed the word, *later*.

Once Tom was finished with his order he walked closer to Joni. "Do you want a drink, love?"

"I would love a mineral water, please."

Tom added ice and a slice of lemon to a cold glass, held the tap over the glass, and filled it before pushing it close to her.

"Thanks."

"You're welcome. You want anything, Gabe?"

"Cola."

Tom passed the cola to Gabe and watched as Joni made notes on a pad and then she grabbed her glass and slid off the stool.

"Where are you going?" Gabe asked.

"To talk to Brent. I want to make a few suggestions on how to improve the menu a little."

"He won't like changing the menu, and they cost a lot to print."

"I wasn't going to change the whole menu. In fact I think what he has on here is fine, but most of these are simple pub meals, and there is nothing wrong with that. But if he had a specials board he could add a couple of more upmarket dishes and attract more money into the hotel.

"We can have a special board hung on the wall over there." Joni pointed and Gabe was impressed because the board would be seen from every part of the dining room and also by patrons heading to the bar. "Plus we can have an easel-type blackboard outside on the sidewalk with prices next to the specials. If we can entice people in wanting to treat their taste buds and they know how much it will cost them in advance, I think you will get a lot more customers."

Gabe smiled and nodded. "I love your idea. I'll leave you to speak with Brent."

The cool expression left Joni's face when she smiled back. Tom's breath hitched in his throat and his dick hardened at the passionate sparkle in her eyes. She was a gorgeously beautiful woman, and when she dropped her aloofness, she was captivating and seemed to glow from the inside. He so wanted to tap into that emotion she had buried deep and have it directed his and his friends' way, but she was nowhere near ready yet.

"What happened?" Tom asked as Nic moved up next to him.

"I put my foot in it."

"What did you say?" Nic crossed his arms over his chest.

"We were talking about drinking and food. She thought it was great that we continue to serve snack and finger food after meals are finished. She said there was nothing worse than a drunk with an empty stomach, but there was this tone to her voice. Before I could think about what I was saying, I said 'I hope that's not from experience' and she clammed right up."

"Fuck!" Nic pointed a finger at Gabe. "I hope you haven't ruined our chances with her."

"Nic, calm the hell down." Tom nudged Nic's side with his elbow. "You can't argue when we have customers. You can't accuse

Gabe of anything when she's not even ours yet. Plus, she was more than happy when she left if the smile on her face was any indication."

"Noticed that, too, did you?" Gabe sipped his soda.

Tom nodded and smiled. "That little girl loves it when we praise her so I suggest you start brushing off your compliments and use them as much as possible."

"She was turned on when we were talking about BDSM," Nic stated the obvious.

"Yes, but how do we get her to agree to trying it?" Tom asked.

"She's mistrustful. The only way we can gain her trust is to be honest," Gabe said.

"So what?" Nic raised an eyebrow. "We tell her we are attracted to her and want a ménage BDSM relationship with her?"

"Yes."

"Shit, Gabe. That could very well send her running in the opposite direction."

"I don't think it will," Tom said. "She was unemployed until today. She uses work to circumvent loneliness. Her career is her solace and even though she may refuse us, or laugh in our faces, I don't think she'll ever quit a job unless something really bad happens."

"How would you know that?" Nic asked.

"When you went to the bathroom I called her last employer. This Gerrard guy couldn't praise her enough. He said she was so efficient she was almost machinelike and although he didn't want to let her go, his sister has the controlling percent of shares in the business and threatened to sell her half out from under her brother if he didn't hire her son, his nephew."

"What a bitch?" Nic muttered.

"No doubt." Tom shrugged.

"Does Joni know any of this?"

"Only that he sacked her to give her position to his nephew. Not the reason why."

"We need to tell her," Gabe said.

"I agree." Nic relaxed his stance. "If she knows the reason she was replaced had nothing to do with her, or her abilities, she may relax even more."

"It's certainly worth a try," Tom said.

* * * *

Joni really liked Brent. He sort of felt like the brother she'd never had. She'd rolled her sleeves up, washed her hands, donned an apron, and asked him what he wanted help with.

He'd been surprised but had immediately put her to work chopping and dicing a ten-pound bag of onions. She would have laughed if she hadn't known she was being tested. So without a complaint, she donned the gloves and started. She'd learned to breathe through her mouth while dealing with such pungent bulbs. Although she knew it wouldn't stop her eyes from tearing up eventually it slowed the effects down.

"Have you ever thought about having a specials board for a more developed palate?" Joni asked, hoping Brent didn't get his nose out of joint.

"This is a pub, love, not an *a la carte* restaurant," Brent snorted.

"I know that and I wasn't going to ask you to serve escargot, nor change the menu selection. I just thought it would be nice to entice more people in if you served something more than steak and chicken parmesan. Sometimes people may want to taste something a little more elaborate."

"Like?" Brent checked the dishes of baked cream potatoes and other vegetable dishes his apprentices were putting into the *bains-marie*. He dipped a clean spoon into the sauce and tasted it.

"Great job, Julie. The potato casserole is divine."

"Thanks, Brent," Julie replied.

Joni sniffed and wiped her face on both of her shoulders. The onion fumes were starting to get to her and she didn't want any of her tears landing on the food.

"What about fresh seafood platters?"

"We already offer seafood platters." Brent turned to look at her with a frown.

"Yes, and no doubt they taste wonderful, but most of it is fried. What if you offered oysters Kilpatrick or *au naturale*? Smoked oysters, salmon, crayfish, and fresh prawns? You could up the price and make more of a profit."

"You know, that's not such a bad idea, but how will we get the people inside? Most people who come here know the menu never changes."

"I will buy one of those easel-type double blackboards, write the specials on it and the price of each dish. That way people can decide if they want to pay a little more for better quality, healthier food and hopefully it will entice more people to enter."

Brent had been frowning at her but a slow smile spread across his face. "I like you, Joni Meeks. You have a good head for business."

"Thanks, I used to work at Gerrard's Restaurant."

"I know the place and I know Gerrard. Not very well, of course, but he seems nice enough. I had just finished my apprenticeship when he opened up. I was a couple of weeks too late to apply for a job there, but he struggled for a few years to gain a reputation." Brent looked at her speculatively. "When did you start working there?"

"Five years ago."

"That explains everything."

"What does?" Joni asked.

"That place started picking up all of a sudden, and if my guess is correct it was approximately five years ago. Am I right?"

Joni smiled and nodded. She wasn't being boastful but knew her suggestions and management had headed Gerrard's Restaurant in the right direction. She'd been studying all about the hospitality industry when she was working and had applied everything she'd learned, and to her surprise it had worked.

"Why did you leave?" Brent asked.

"Gerrard fired me?"

"What the fuck for?" Brent yelled.

"He wanted to hire his nephew because he'd just finished college."

"What an ass! Don't take it to heart, Joni. From what I've heard around the traps, his sister owns just over half of that place."

"So you think she tugged on the cash strings?"

"She did," Tom said.

Joni glanced over her shoulder and looked through moisture-filled eyes at Tom. He frowned and then hurried over until he was standing beside her.

"No wonder you're crying. Did you peel and chop all those onions?"

Joni wiped her cheeks on her shoulder again and sniffed before nodding. She chopped the last onion and after getting rid of the peels, took the chopping board and knife to the sink to rinse them. She removed the gloves, dumped them in the trash, and washed her hands.

"Don't give me that look." Brent held his hands up in a supplicatory gesture. "She offered to help."

"I did, so get that look off your face right now, Tom." Joni planted her hands on her hips, but her nose started to run so she had to spin away and grab some tissues from the shelf to blow it. She hated that she turned away from him when she was standing up for Brent and herself, but she didn't want snot running down her face. She threw the tissues in the trash, washed her hands once more, and, after she dried them on a paper towel, turned to face Tom again.

She was surprised to see him looking at her with a goofy smile on his face, but it was the heat in his eyes that gave her pause. At first she thought she was imagining things but when he ran his gaze up and down her body before meeting her eyes again, she couldn't refute what was right in front of her face.

"You are so sexy when you're obstinate."

"Huh…"

Brent burst out laughing. "You should see your face, Joni. You look like you've just seen a ghost or something."

Joni turned her glare on Brent, but with him smiling at her that way she couldn't hold her ire or a straight face and ended up smiling again. She couldn't remember the last time she'd smiled with anyone other than Kara, and now it seemed her bosses could illicit such from her with just a few words of praise, and Brent's laughter was just downright contagious.

"Yeah, yeah, everyone's a comedian," she muttered and then pointed to the large bowl of diced onions. "I'll leave you and your minions to deal with that. I need to check out the bar."

"Thanks Joni," Brent called. "I'll have a specials menu to you tomorrow and we can start implementing it as soon as possible."

"Okay."

Joni hurried toward the bar and was pleasantly surprised to see the place was filling up. There were a couple of EMTs in uniform standing at the bar, sipping on beers while talking to Nic and Gabe as they continued to serve. She didn't want to get in their way but she needed to make sure the BOM matched the inventory. She'd already taken the time to copy files over to her tablet so she could check things off her list and then she needed to look in the cellar or storage room, whatever the case may be.

The smiles Gabe and Nic gave her made her warm inside and even though she didn't want to, she found herself smiling back. When she realized she stood behind the bar staring at them all, she gave herself a mental shake and got back to work.

By the time she was done and made sure that the inventory matched the list, the place was full. Tom worked behind the bar with his friends and since they were so busy, Joni decided to search for their storage room by herself.

She walked along the hall toward the office and noticed a door farther along from the kitchen but before the back door exit. She turned the knob and sighed with relief when it opened. She didn't want to have to go back and ask for a key when the others were so busy. Because it was so dark she pulled her cell phone from her pocket and used the illumination from it to find a light switch. She was very glad she had because there were about five stairs leading into a basement-type cellar room. She spent the next few hours checking everything off her list and when she was done, she sighed with tiredness. When she glanced at the time on her tablet she noticed it was already after 10 p.m. No wonder she was so tired. She'd been here for over twelve hours.

Joni hurried up the stairs and headed back to the bar. Since it was Friday night there were still a lot of patrons and she wondered what time they closed the door. If she was lucky, she would be able to leave in another two hours. If not, maybe another three. It depended on their liquor license.

As she slid onto a vacant stool near the end of the bar, Nic approached and, from the look on his face, he wasn't happy. "Where the hell have you been? We've been searching all over for you and thought you'd left."

"I was in the cellar room checking off the stock against the BOM."

"Why didn't you let one of us know where you were?" Nic asked angrily.

"Because you were busy and I didn't want to bother you."

"First rule, you let us know where you are at all times." Nic glared at her, shifted on his feet, and crossed his arms over his chest.

Joni didn't like his attitude or the way he was acting like a father and treating her like a child.

"Get over yourself, Nic."

Gabe must have heard what both of them had said because he hurried over and placed a restraining hand on Nic's shoulder, who then uncrossed his arms and leaned on the bar, which brought him close to her. "Both of you need to back off. This isn't the time for heated discussions. You can wait until we close."

Joni sighed with guilt. She didn't usually jump down someone's throat without thinking first, but she was tired and she had been nursing a headache for the last hour and it seemed to be getting worse with each second that passed. She glanced from Gabe to Nic and then offered a tentative smile. "I'm sorry. I don't usually snap like that."

Nic pushed up straight, his gaze scrutinizing her face and then he frowned. "What's wrong?"

"Nothing."

She looked to the side and was pleased that all the clients who'd been waiting for drinks had had their orders filled and had moved away from the bar. Tom walked over to stand beside Gabe and she was disconcerted with the way all three of them were staring at her so intently. Although she tried to keep her desire under wraps, it didn't seem to make a difference. Her body didn't take one damn bit of notice of her brain. She wanted all three of them but that was never going to happen. She would make sure of that. But how was she going to continue hiding how horny they made her?

She drew in a breath, raised her arms, and crossed them over her breasts, trying to hide her hard, aching nipples from view. When her arms brushed against the sensitive tips she had to bite her lip and swallow back a moan of hunger.

"You're exhausted," Tom said, drawing her gaze. "I think you should call it a night."

Gabe glanced at his wristwatch and winced. "Fuck! I had no idea what the damn time was. You've been here for over twelve fucking hours."

"Shit!" Nic threaded his fingers through his hair. "No wonder you're looking so pale. Are you sure you're just tired? You don't look so great, baby."

Joni was starting to feel like crap warmed up, but she wasn't about to show weakness in front of these three authoritative, confident, dominant men. She had a feeling if she gave an inch they'd run roughshod right over the top of her, and she'd never get any ground back. "I'm fine."

Gabe frowned at her and she decided she would take them up on finishing up. The more her head ached, the more her stomach roiled. Joni hoped she was coming down with something, because although she got the occasional headache she was lucky enough to not suffer migraines. But the headache she had now was like a drum pounding on the inside of her skull and she felt a little achy and light-headed. She slid from the stool and gripped the edge of the bar when her world tilted slightly. She blinked a couple of times and sighed with relief when her vision came back. When she straightened up she met three pairs of very concerned eyes.

"There is no way in hell you're driving home," Gabe stated emphatically. "You're about ready to pass out."

"I'll be fine," Joni replied as she began to make her way toward the office where she'd left her purse and cardigan. She shivered as the air from the vent above her head washed over her body. Goose bumps raced over her skin and she shuddered, feeling a bone-deep coldness. She didn't get more than five feet before she slammed into a hard muscular body.

Hands grasped her hips and steadied her and it hurt her head and neck when she looked up to meet Nic's concerned gaze. "I'll drive you home, Joni."

"But—" She didn't get to say anything else because he interrupted her.

"No arguing. There is no way I'm letting you drive home in your state. You could have a car accident and I couldn't live with my conscience if you ended up in a car wreck."

Joni was too tired to argue, plus she agreed with him. The way she was feeling it would be a miracle if she got home. "Thank you."

He shifted away and then gripped her elbow, guiding her down the hallway and into the office. After she retrieved her things, she let him guide her back out to the front and, after saying good-bye to Gabe and Tom, he led her to his car.

"Where do you live, baby?"

Joni rolled her head on the headrest and squinted at him before rattling off her address. She hated that he would see the dump of a building she lived in, but he wouldn't get to see the small space she leased because she had no intentions of asking him in for coffee. Although now that that thought had rolled across her mind, it was on the tip of her tongue to do just that, but she sighed and closed her eyes instead.

She hoped that if she was getting sick it passed quickly because she couldn't afford to take anytime off when she'd just started. Oh well, it didn't really matter how she felt. She'd gone to work sick plenty of times. As long as she dosed herself up with flu medication or whatever she needed she would be fine. It didn't matter if she were tired, she'd gotten by on little-to-no sleep plenty of times.

Although she didn't go to sleep, she had her eyes closed and sort of drifted while Nic drove. It was only when she no longer heard the tires on the road or engine noise that she realized they had stopped. When she opened her eyes, it was to find Nic's eyes running over her face as if he was tracing every one of her features until he got to her eyes.

Her heart stuttered in her chest and her breath hitched in her throat at the lust she saw in his gaze. Joni blinked and sat up, pushing the few strands of hair which had escaped her bun back, and reached for the door handle. Nic clasped her other wrist and she turned back to face him.

"Stay right where you are, Joni," he commanded. "I'll help you out."

If she hadn't been feeling under the weather she may have argued, but she just didn't have the energy. He released her wrist, got out, hurried around to her side of the car, and helped her out. When she stood, instead of stepping back, he wrapped an arm around her waist, sidestepped her a couple of paces, and then closed and locked the door before guiding her to the door of her ground floor one-bedroom apartment.

She cringed when she saw a couple of garbage bags off the sidewalk and when she looked up at the dilapidated building she felt embarrassed. She hadn't really cared what others thought about where she lived, but for some reason having Nic see her rundown apartment made her feel bad.

The path lights were out and when she squinted through the couple of bushes near her front door, she saw that her external entrance light was out, too. At first she thought there may have been a power outage but when she looked toward the apartments on either side of hers and saw light on each side of the drawn curtains, and blinds, she knew she was wrong. There was always something needing to be fixed and she knew from experience that the so-called caretaker of maintenance wouldn't get off his lazy, fat ass to do anything.

If she wanted to be able to see her keyhole she was going to have to get a new light globe and change it out herself. The closer they got to her place the more she shivered and it wasn't because she wasn't feeling up to par. She felt like she was being watched and didn't like the way the feeling creeped her out. After glancing about, she couldn't see anyone lurking in the shadows but she couldn't shake the sensation of eyes watching her every move. She sighed with relief when she and Nic got to her door and, after fumbling with the key in the lock, she managed to get it in and opened the door.

Joni felt along the wall for the light switch and when the room illuminated she stood in shock as her eyes swept the room. The secondhand sofa she'd managed to recover was slashed to ribbons with stuffing sticking out and spilling onto the floor. The wooden coffee table she'd made and painted with her own hands was in pieces and the small collection of ex-rental DVDs she splurged on were scattered about in shiny shards. She heard Nic growl beside her and even though she wanted to turn and look at him, she couldn't.

It took her a few moments to realize she was shaking and that was why everything seemed to be moving slightly and just as she was about to rush across the debris littering the floor, Nic cupped her face in his hands and met her eyes.

"Take a deep breath, baby." His quiet command helped calm some of the panic rushing through her system and she was able to take the first deep breath since the moment she'd walked in the door. "Good girl, that's it, Joni. Keep breathing with me."

How long they stood there as he talked her from the anxiety rushing through her she had no idea, but finally her racing heart came back to a nearly normal pace and she was no longer panting as if she'd just run her heart out.

"Come on," Nic murmured as he released her face and took hold of one of her hands. "You need to sit in the truck."

"No." Joni shook her head and pulled away from him and the wall she'd been leaning on. She ignored him and hurried across the small living area to her bedroom.

"Joni!" Nic's voice was harsh but again she didn't take any notice. She needed to see her bedroom. She had no idea why the compunction drove her, but she couldn't ignore it.

She turned the light on and her stomach muscles heaved when she saw what was left of her bed and clothes. Absolutely nothing had survived the onslaught of destruction. The mattress had been ripped to shreds and the springs had been half pulled out. Her clothes were in pieces or slashed. Even the two other pairs of shoes she had hadn't avoided ruination. When she caught movement from the corner of her eye, fear skittered up her spine, but she exhaled as she saw that it was the curtains fluttering in the breeze. That was when she saw her bedroom window was no more. It had been broken and glass was lying on the floor.

"Do you have any idea who would do this?" Nic asked in an angry voice.

Joni had been so caught up in staring in shock she hadn't been aware that he'd followed her. She glanced at him and shook her head and then she started picking her way through the destruction. She picked up the lace white shawl that had belonged to her mother and a knot of grief and pain formed in her chest. Although it was still one piece, it had been cut several times and would need to be thrown away. She dropped it back on the floor and covered her mouth to hold in the sobs building in her chest.

She had no idea why anyone would to this and didn't think she had upset anyone to cause such hatred and anger. As far as she knew, she had no enemies and wondered if this was just a random attack for someone to get their jollies.

"You can't stay here, Joni. You can stay with us." Nic rubbed her shoulder and even though she felt his touch, it was like she was experiencing things from a long way off. Nothing seemed real. How could any of this be real when she'd never crossed anyone? She'd always been polite no matter what. Her momma had brought her up to be nice to everyone, no matter how pissed off they made her. She'd even held her tongue when Gerrard had fired her after making his business what it was today, just so he could employ his nephew.

Joni's head began pounding worse than ever before and she was so cold she was shivering. She was only vaguely aware of Nic talking on his cell phone but none of his words were comprehensible. Her legs felt weak and no matter how hard she tried to stop trembling, it only seemed to make it worse.

Pinpricks of dark spots formed in front of her eyes and no amount of blinking removed them. She tried to see where Nic was but the darkness grew until there was nothing to see but black. With a sigh of relief, she gave in and drifted away.

Chapter Six

"Shit!" Nic dropped his cell and grabbed Joni just as her legs buckled. He lifted her into his arms and then crouched to pick up his phone from the floor before standing again. "Hang on a minute," he yelled so Gabe would hear him.

He didn't want to put her on the wrecked bed or the ruined sofa so he strode out of her apartment and hurried toward his truck. He managed to get his keys from his pocket and after unlocking the door, eased Joni onto the backseat. He snagged his jacket from where he'd placed on the back of the driver's seat and covered her up.

When he had her settled he put his phone to his ear. "You need to get over here. Someone's trashed her place."

"Have you called the cops?"

"Yeah, Gary Wade is on his way. She passed out, Gabe."

"Fuck! We'll be there in ten."

Nic disconnected the call. He hadn't taken his eyes off of Joni, but he didn't like how pale she was. Every now and then she whimpered in her sleep as if she were in pain. His heart seized and he drew a deep breath. He hated seeing her like this and wanted to do something to make her feel better, but he had no idea what was wrong other than her decimated home and wondered if he should call an ambulance or a doctor. He hoped that Jack Williams was with Gary, since he was a doctor.

Headlights coming toward him drew his attention and when the vehicle pulled in behind his truck he saw that it was Gary and he had his friends and his wife with him. Relief coursed through his body knowing he could rely on Jack to examine Joni.

"Thanks for coming," Nic greeted and shook each man's hand before kissing their wife, Emma, on the cheek.

"Is she all right?" Emma asked when she spied Joni out of it on the backseat.

"I don't know." He turned to Jack. "Can you look her over, please? She wasn't looking so good earlier and that's why I drove her home. I think she was suffering from shock when she passed out. She was shaking like a leaf before her legs buckled."

Jack nodded, hurried toward their truck, and came back with his medical bag in hand. "Emma, can you get in back with her? I don't want her getting scared if she wakes up while I'm looking her over."

"Of course," Emma turned away but then spun back. "What's the lady's name, Nic?"

"Joni. Joni Meeks."

Emma nodded and then walked around to the other door and got into the back. Jack pulled his stethoscope from his bag and got to work.

"So what happened?" Gary asked.

Nic explained and Gary nodded every now and then as they walked back to Joni's apartment.

"Fucking hell." Gary frowned as he looked around. "Someone is very angry with that little lady."

"Yeah, but why?" Nic asked.

"I was hoping you could answer that question."

Nic shrugged. "Joni has no idea either."

"Could be the work of a psychopath, but this definitely looks personal."

Nic turned when he heard more footsteps heading their way and watched as Gabe and Tom entered the small, one-bedroom apartment.

"Geezus." Tom scrubbed a hand down his face.

"What the fuck?" Gabe spat, his eyes taking in the demolished room.

"I've called forensics," Gary said and he got off the phone. "If Jack's finished looking the woman over, why don't you take her back to your place? I'll come by first thing in the morning to talk to her."

Nic nodded and, after saying good-bye, headed out to his truck. He was pleased to see Joni sitting up in the backseat, but she was still awfully pale.

Jack moved away from his truck and, after making sure Joni was comfortable with Emma, Nic walked over to stand next to him.

"She's dehydrated and has a bad headache, but other than that she's fine."

"Thank god." Nic sighed.

"She's a bit achy and needs to rest and replenish her fluids but should be fine after a good night's sleep."

"Good," Gabe said, shaking Jack's hand. "We'll take her home and get her into bed."

"If you have any other concerns, give me a call."

"Thanks, Jack."

Jack waved and went to help Emma from the backseat of his truck. Nic moved to the open door and took Joni's hand in his. He didn't like that her skin felt icy cold.

"We're taking you to our place, Joni." He held up his other hand when she opened her mouth, no doubt to protest. "You can't stay here, baby. Until we know what's going on we want to make sure you're safe."

Joni shivered and nodded at the same time. He saw relief in her eyes and knew the thought of staying in her home scared her and was glad she'd acquiesced to him.

"Do you want to stay where you are, or do you want to sit up front?"

Joni licked her dry lips and when she answered he had to strain to hear her. "Front."

He nodded and, without waiting for her to get out, reached in and lifted her into his arms. Gabe hurried to the front passenger door and opened it for him. He gently placed her on the seat and helped her buckle up.

"We'll see you at home." Gabe and Tom strode toward Tom's truck.

Nic started the truck and pulled out onto the road. He drove in silence but could feel the tension emanating from his passenger. He wanted to put her at ease but knew nothing he said right now would wipe the scene of her apartment from her mind. "Joni, do you think you previous boss could do something like this?"

She turned to face him but shook her head. "No. Gerrard was an ass but he wouldn't do something like…"

When he heard her sob he looked over to see that she'd covered her mouth with her hand and tears were rolling down her face. He'd never been so glad that his truck had been fitted out with a bench seat and not two separate ones.

"Oh, baby. I'm sorry for what happened to your things." He pushed the button on her safety belt, releasing it, and tugged on her hand after clasping it. "Come over here, Joni."

He was glad when Joni didn't hesitate and scooted over next to him. He released her hand and tugged the lap belt from under her ass and then lifted it over her lap. "Put your belt on, baby. I don't want you getting hurt."

She fumbled until she had the belt buckled and then he slung an arm over her shoulders and drew her closer. He held in his sigh of relief when she didn't protest and in actual fact pressed her cheek against his chest. Her shoulders were shaking and although she tried to contain her sobs, he still heard them.

"Let it go, Joni. Don't try and hold all that pain inside, baby. It'll eat you up if you do." His words seemed to be the catalyst because she started sobbing uncontrollably. He hated that she was hurting but hoped that by releasing her emotions it would be cathartic and help her heal.

He stroked her arm, shoulder, and head but when her tears didn't seem to be slowing any he got real concerned, but guessed she had a load of emotions roiling around inside of her that had nothing to do with tonight's horrific events.

Nic hated the way his body responded to her closeness, his dick hardening and twitching in his pants when the time was so inappropriate, but he just couldn't seem to control his body's response whenever she was close, and having her plastered up against him was doing his head in. She smelled so nice and fit perfectly against his harder frame and although the urge to stop the truck and kiss her was almost too much to ignore, ignore it he did.

Finally, he pulled into the drive and cut the engine before releasing his and her seatbelts, and then he lifted her up onto his lap. Since she now had her head buried in his chest he couldn't see if she was still crying but from the occasional hiccup wracking her body, he determined that she had at least slowed her jag.

"It's okay, baby. Everything will be all right," Nic crooned in a low, soothing voice.

"I'm sorry," she croaked as she placed her hands on his chest and pushed back to look him in the eyes.

She was so damn beautiful, even with her eyes bloodshot and her nose red from her fit of crying. The urge to kiss her was so strong he had to take a few deep breaths and slowly exhale to control the craving. She'd been through enough tonight and didn't need him mauling her after such a horrendous shock.

"You okay?"

"Yeah."

"Good." He opened the door and carefully lifted her up into his arms and slid out of his seat, making sure he didn't bump her on the steering wheel. She surprised him when she hooked her arms around his neck and rested her head on his shoulder with a shuddering sigh, just as Gabe and Tom pulled up.

"She okay?" Gabe asked as he hurried over.

"I'm fine," Joni answered without lifting her head.

"Of course you are, honey, but you have to be beyond exhausted." Gabe stroked a hand over her head and down, unraveling the bun.

Nic drew in a deep awed breath at the length of her luxurious tresses. She was even more beautiful than he suspected. His dick filled with blood and fully engorged, making him uncomfortable but again he ignored his body's yearning.

"I am," Joni answered and then sighed.

"Bring her in," Tom called from the front porch and Nic started walking toward the door. Hopefully after Joni was rested she wouldn't look so pale and shell-shocked and if he had any say in it, she wouldn't be starting work before lunchtime tomorrow. He just hoped she was a heavy sleeper and didn't hear them get up in the morning. He and his buddies had always been early rises, no matter what time they went to sleep or how long they slept for. They were going to have to keep quiet and not be their normal, raucous selves.

Nic carried her down the hall, skirting to the side when Gabe rushed ahead of him and opened the door to the master bedroom. He quirked his eyebrow at his friend, knowing the significance of the bedroom choice when they had another spare guest room they could put Joni in, but he nodded in agreement and smiled as he stepped over the threshold.

Joni didn't know it yet but as far as they were concerned she was theirs and he was going to do everything he could to make sure she was comfortable and never wanted to leave. He knew it wouldn't happen overnight but he wanted her to have feelings for them, the same way they had feelings for her. He wasn't a green youth and knew his own mind. He knew that Joni was special. Now all he and his friends needed to do was convince her of that, too.

But that sounded a lot easier than he suspected it was going to be.

* * * *

Anger coursed through Paul's body until a red haze formed in front of his eyes. He had broken into Joni's apartment hoping to scare her into seeking him out for comfort.

When he'd seen that other fucker with her he'd wanted to roar with fury. She was supposed to be his. He'd done everything he could to get her attention but nothing he'd done had worked. And now it looked like he was too late.

He'd never thought Joni was like all the other sluts he'd been with. He'd thought she was innocent and special, but it looked like he was wrong.

She was going to pay for ignoring him. No one ignored Paul Farris and got away with it.

No one.

She was going to be his whether she wanted to or not and when he got hold of her he was going to make her pay.

* * * *

Tom hurried into the room after Nic and helped Gabe pull the covers back on the bigger than king-size custom-made bed. When Nic lowered Joni onto the mattress, she sighed and rolled over onto her side. Her eyes were closed but he could tell by the puffy lids that she'd been crying. He brushed the hair off her face and then pulled the covers up to her shoulders after Nic removed her shoes. She was so beautiful and even though she was no longer crying he had a feeling she had years' worth of stored up pain locked inside of her.

If she gave them a chance to have a relationship with her they could set her free, but first they had to get her to agree. Without thinking about what he was doing, he bent down and pressed his lips to her forehead. He drew in the light scent she wore and held it in his lungs before exhaling and straightening up again.

She sighed and the corner of her lips curved up in a slight smile. Seeing her reaction to a simple kiss on her head gave him hope that she would indeed accept him and his friends. Giving her one last longing look, he turned and followed Nic and Gabe out to the kitchen.

"She's been crying," Tom said as he accepted the bottle of beer from Gabe and took a slug from it.

"Yeah," Nic sighed. "She's been to hell and back tonight and although she tried to keep her sobs in, she was fighting a losing battle."

"She was definitely in shock," Gabe said. "Who wouldn't after coming home to such a mess? Joni probably feels violated at the way her things were destroyed."

"Does she have any idea who would want to hurt her like that?" Tom asked.

"No," Nic answered.

"Damn. I hope Gary and the forensics team find some prints to go on." Gabe ran his fingers through his hair.

"We'll have to try and keep it down in the morning. I want her to sleep for as long as possible," Nic said.

"Do you think we should let her work tomorrow?" Gabe muttered and then held up his hand before Tom or Nic replied. "Don't bother answering that. I know she'd put up a fuss if we suggested she take the day off."

"You're right about that," Nic agreed.

"She's so different at work than when we met her at the club the other night," Tom said.

"Yes, she is. She was so far out of her comfort zone she was virtually vibrating with nerves." Gabe sipped his beer.

"Yes, but although she was nervous, she was also turned on." Nic leaned against the kitchen counter.

"So, do you think we should tell her what we want with her?" Tom asked the question that his friends no doubt had rolling around in their minds.

"It's too early," Gabe said. "We need to give her more time to get used to us. Make sure you touch her often, but not inappropriately.

Talk with her, joke and laugh with her but give her some space for now. There's no way she can go back home until whoever broke in and is after her, is caught."

"We don't know for sure that she's in danger." Tom glanced toward the door, before meeting Nic's and Gabe's gazes again. "For all we know it could have been a random attack."

"Do you really believe that?" Gabe frowned.

"No." Tom sighed. "None of the walls or curtains were destroyed. It was all her things."

"It was personal." Nic slammed his fist into the counter, his teeth clenched, making the muscle in his jaw twitch.

"That settles it, then." Gabe nodded. "She's not going home."

"She'll put up a fight." Tom couldn't stop himself smiling at the thought.

"Yes, and I'm looking forward to it as much as you are." Nic pointed his finger at Tom.

"We'd better head to bed and get some shut-eye." Gabe drained the last of his beer and then tossed the empty bottle into the recycle bin. "We're going to need to have our wits about us tomorrow."

Tom nodded, said good night, and headed to his room. As far as he was concerned tomorrow couldn't come fast enough.

Chapter Seven

Joni sighed and blinked open blurry eyes. She frowned when she noted she wasn't in her bedroom and sat up with bewilderment. When she looked down and realized she'd slept in her clothes, the previous night's events came rushing back. She covered her face with her hands and groaned when she remembered blubbering all over Nic. Embarrassment heated her face and although she remembered being in his truck she didn't remember much after her crying jag.

"God, Joni! Could you make yourself look more of a fool?" As she finished muttering that question, she realized that she'd liked being held by Nic, and not just because she felt safe, protected. Whenever she was around him, Gabe, and Tom her libido sat up and took notice. And now she was supposed to be staying with them for however long it took to catch whoever had broken in and trashed her things. How was she supposed to keep her attraction to them hidden if she was living with them? She'd had virtually no experience with the opposite sex through choices of her own and wasn't sure if they had a hidden agenda by wanting to help her out. From her involvement with men all they ever wanted to do was cause pain. She'd had enough of that to last her a lifetime and didn't want to ever have to go through something so agonizing again.

John had never really taken any time with her in the bedroom. All he ever did was grope her a couple of times before sticking his dick into her and thrusting until he got off. She'd thought there had been something wrong with her because that asshole had keep telling her she was a cold emotionless bitch. And stupid her, she had believed him. She'd been so damn naïve and sometimes she hated herself for her gullibility. From the conversations she'd had with Kara there was so much more to sex than what she'd experienced but she wasn't about to get that close to another man again.

And then there was her father.

Joni blinked back the tears that threatened whenever she thought of her mom and her sick asshole of a father, but when she realized she was getting morbid and having a self-pity party, she pushed her depressing thoughts aside.

Nothing could change the past but she could damn well control her future.

She pushed the covers aside and hurried toward the adjoining bathroom. Maybe after a hot shower she would feel more herself. Besides, she always had her work. Her career had been the one constant in her life and she clung to it like the lifeline it had become. Working was what kept her sane. If she didn't have that she was scared she would break apart and never be able to put the pieces back together again.

After her shower, she wrapped a large fluffy towel around her body, brushed her wet hair, and braided it to keep it out of the way. Joni loved her hair and, although she got it trimmed twice a year and often thought about cutting the weight off, she'd never been brave enough to do something so drastic. Her mom used to spend a long time brushing the tangles out and Joni had cherished the quiet moments as her mother's lilac scent and touch of her hands portrayed the love she had for her. She missed those times and even though she was lonely, she endured, taking each day one step at a time.

When she comprehended where her thoughts were drifting again, she blanked her mind, brushed her teeth, and then entered the bedroom. She froze in her tracks when she saw Gabe sitting on the edge of the bed.

"How are you feeling, honey?" He stood and walked toward her.

Joni crossed her arms over her chest when her nipples pebbled and shifted on her feet when her pussy began to ache. She met his eyes briefly before her gaze skittered away. "I'm fine. Thanks."

"I brought you some clothes." Gabe pointed to the bundle on the end of the bed. "One of us will take you shopping later. Breakfast is ready and waiting for when you're dressed."

Joni bit back a whimper when he stroked a finger down her cheek. His nostrils flared and his pupils dilated and she had a feeling he could see what her body was doing, but she tried to keep her face expressionless.

"Don't take too long, honey. You don't want the food to get cold."

She shivered when his finger caressed over her shoulder and down her bare arm and just as she parted her lips to moan, he turned and hurried away, closing the door behind him. Joni sank down onto the edge of the bed, her legs trembling and weak, making her unsure if they would hold her up any longer. When her thighs brushed against each other she felt moisture on her upper legs as they slid with slickness and Joni knew she was in deep shit. But what concerned her most was their dominant tendencies. If she got involved with them, would she lose herself because they ruled over her?

That was one of the reasons her mom had left her father. He'd been so controlling, picking on her about every little thing and in the end he'd never let her go anywhere unless he was by her side. Joni had been so scared of her dad because every time he opened his mouth it was to yell at her mom and in the end, he ended up beating on her. That had been the last straw for her mom and they'd left.

Could she trust her growing feelings for these three men? Could she trust them not to hurt her even when they wanted to hit her? Joni shook her head. There was no way she could get involved with them. What she should be doing was leaving and heading back home, but for some reason she just couldn't make herself do that.

When she was dressed in the borrowed sweats and sweater, which she'd had to roll down and up in appropriate places so they wouldn't fall off or swim on her, she headed out to the kitchen.

Nic looked up when she entered and walked toward her. "You okay?"

She nodded, keeping her head down, hoping he wouldn't see how embarrassed she was over falling apart on him last night.

"Look at me, Joni," he commanded in a quiet, yet firm voice and she found herself complying with his demand. "Don't be ashamed of feeling, baby. You had every right to cry last night."

She nodded and would have stepped around him but he placed a hand on her shoulder and she found herself meeting his eyes. He gently pulled her into his arms and pulled her up against his body. She closed her eyes and breathed in his wonderful sandalwood and masculine scent and melted against him. She just couldn't seem to help herself and wanted to stay wrapped up in his warmth and comfort for the rest of her life.

Joni stiffened and felt the blood drain from her face as that thought coalesced. She pulled away and hurried over to the table and sat down. When Tom placed a mug of coffee in front of her, she lifted trembling hands and wrapped her cold flesh around the warm cup.

"Joni, what's wrong?" Tom asked.

She shook her head and pressed her lips together and tried not to flinch when Tom clasped her chin between his finger and thumb. But she wasn't flinching because he scared her. The complete opposite, in fact. She liked the way they touched her and didn't know what to do about it. "I need to go home," she blurted out.

"Not happening, Joni," Gabe said in a hard voice. "Until we know who the hell is after you, you'll be staying here."

"And how long will that be? I have no idea who did that to my place. For all I know it was a drug addict looking for money or stuff to sell."

"Do you really think an addict would cut up your clothes?" Tom frowned.

Joni shrugged as if she didn't care, when inside she quaked with fear. She wasn't stupid and knew that someone had it in for her, but for the life of her she couldn't figure out who. She'd never done anything wrong and hadn't made any enemies. Not any that she knew of anyway.

The only person she could think of was her father but that couldn't be possible because he was locked away in an institution for the rest of his life.

"Detective Gary Wade will be here any minute. He's a friend and I can tell you now he won't want you going back home where you'll be in danger," Nic explained. "Do you have anyone else you can stay with?"

Joni was about to nod but for some reason she found it really hard to lie to these men and her damn body betrayed her by shaking her head. She sighed with resignation and frustration when she finally lifted her head and glanced at all three of them. They had their arms crossed over their chests and there was dogged determination in their eyes. She had a feeling the only way she was leaving was if she snuck out.

"Don't even think about it." Gabe pointed his finger at her and gave her a fierce look. That dominant action sent her body into haywire. She drew in a ragged breath when her nipples hardened even more, if that were possible, and her pussy throbbed and clenched, drenching the sweatpants.

"I don't have to do what you tell me to." Joni cringed when her voice came out all breathless and soft, as if she didn't believe the words she'd just spoken. "I'm not a child." This time she spoke forcefully. Thank god she'd found a little backbone.

What was it about these men that made her want to lie down with her throat exposed? She'd never been a pushover before, so why was now so different?

"Oh believe me, baby, we all know how much of a woman you are."

Joni met Nic's eyes and her heart stuttered when she met his potently desirous gaze. And just like that she felt like she was drowning in his brown, hungry eyes. She was hardly aware of him moving closer to her as his chair scraped on the tile floor. Her lids lowered to half-mast when the palm of his hands cupped both her cheeks and she couldn't help staring at his mouth when he licked his lips.

Whether she blinked, she was uncertain, but in the next instant his lips were on hers. Her lips parted on a sigh and then she moaned as his tongue glided along and twirled around hers. Her body heated from the inside, liquid desire running through her veins until she felt as insubstantial as jelly, but excitement coursed through her, too, making her tense.

Her hands lifted and then she was clutching at Nic's shirt as the heat simmering inside began to rage out of control. She felt like she was burning alive and yet she didn't feel any pain, only a deep aching throb inside that was pleasurable. Warm, large, strong fingers pried her own from the shirt she was gripping and then her wrists were grasped and her arms were pushed behind her back.

She whimpered with delight as those hands brought her wrists together and shackled them in one large, firm yet surprisingly gentle grip. Because of the hold she was in, her chest was pushed out and her achingly hard nipples brushed against a warm cotton-covered chest, and it didn't seem to matter that she also had a sweatshirt on. Each brush ramped up the ache and the yearning to have her nipples touched to appease the throbbing was so insistent she tried to pull her hands free to do it herself.

The hand holding her wrists tightened as if in warning and she relaxed, but pressed her chest out even more and sighed with relief when the pressure on her nipples eased the throbbing slightly.

He tasted so damn good she wanted to kiss him until her lips were sore and her jaw ached. When he curled his tongue around hers and sucked it into his mouth she mewled and sighed and gave herself over to him. She wanted, *needed,* for him to do whatever he wanted with her. She wanted him controlling her body, her responses, but most of all she wanted his hands on her.

Nic broke the kiss and rested his forehead on hers and she blinked, slowly coming out of the sexual stupor she'd been in. Joni couldn't believe she'd just let Nic kiss her, let alone kiss him back as if she was starving for him. She moved back and tugged her hands from his hold and hated the way her face heated with mortification, and knew her face would be so pink she probably looked like she was sunburnt.

"Joni, look at me," Nic commanded.

She shook her head and blinked back the tears of shame, but one leaked from the corner of her eye and spilled down her cheek. She flinched when a hand snapped out and peered up when the pregnant silence become too fraught to ignore.

"I was going to tug on your braid," Nic said in a soft, raspy voice. "I would never, ever hit a woman, child, or you." He pushed his chair back, rose to his feet, and began pacing. "Who the hell hurt you, Joni?"

"No one," she answered and reached for her nearly cold coffee, before taking a sip. When her eyes alighted on the food her stomach rolled and the thought of eating made her feel sick.

"That was a blatant lie," Gabe snapped.

She tried to ignore him but should have known he wouldn't allow it. She looked up when he stood and then he was squatting down in front of her, and he placed a hand on her thigh. She shivered and cursed mentally when she saw him watching her and knew he'd seen her telltale reaction.

"Joni, we are all very attracted to you and you can deny it until you're blue in the face, but we know you feel the attraction, too. We want the chance to have a relationship with you. We could give you so much pleasure, honey."

She opened her mouth to say what, she didn't know, but Gabe placed a finger over her lips and halted her before she could speak.

"I don't want you say anything right now. Just think about what I've said. We would never take from you what you aren't willing to give, so don't ever be afraid of us or what you're feeling.

"But if you decide you want to explore this thing between all of us, you are going to have to tell us everything, Joni. That means no secrets. You will tell us what you're feeling when we ask.

"For a relationship to work between a sub and Doms there has to be total trust. Do you understand?"

Once more she opened her mouth and again she didn't know what she was going to say, but she sighed with relief when the doorbell sounded. She'd just been saved by the bell, literally and figuratively.

Gabe muttered a curse, rose to his feet, and hurried from the room. Nic moved his chair away from hers a little and sat before reaching for the now cool food and, without a word, grabbed a piece of toast and topped it with lukewarm eggs.

"You're not leaving the table until you've finished eating that." Nic pointed at her plate and gave her an authoritative stare.

Joni had the childish urge to poke her tongue out at him but didn't want to pull the tiger by the tail. She picked up her knife and fork and, after the first bite hit her tongue, her stomach rumbled. Although it wasn't very hot anymore, it still tasted good and before she knew it she'd cleaned her plate.

She heard voices in the other room just before Gabe and, she presumed, Detective Gary Wade entered. Gabe sat on her other side and Gary sat across from her.

"Joni, this is Detective Gary Wade. Gary, Joni Meeks."

"Hi, Joni, I'm pleased to meet you. I just wish it was under better circumstances," Gary said.

"Me, too."

"So do you have any idea who could have trashed your apartment?"

"No."

"What about an ex?" Gary suggested.

"No," Joni replied immediately. The asshole knew that if he ever came near her again he'd be back in jail, and besides he'd moved clear across to the other side of the country, or so the officer who'd helped her press charges had told her the last time he'd called to see how she was doing. He was a nice man and although she knew they could have been great friends, she'd kept her contact with him to a minimum, not wanting to be reminded of how stupidly naive she'd been. She'd wanted to try and forget that part of her life but knew it was impossible.

"Are you sure? Sometimes guys can get really pissed if they're dumped."

"No."

Gary glanced at Gabe and then back to her. "Gabe told me you were fired from your last job. Does your previous employer have a grudge against you?"

"Not that I know of," she said and then went on to explain why Gerrard had let her go.

"Okay, but I'll still need to check him out."

"Do you have any brothers or sisters?" Gary asked.

"No."

"Parents?"

"N–no."

"Friends?"

"Other than Kara. No."

Gary frowned and Joni didn't know what was going on but all four men looked at each other then back at her. "The forensics team didn't find any prints, so whoever broke in wore gloves. Do you think it could have been any of the other building's residents?"

"It's possible." Joni swallowed nervously.

"Do you know any of the people living in the building?"

"Mr. Rosenberg. I only say hi to the other people in passing. We don't socialize with each other."

"And what apartment does Rosenberg live in?"

"1B, right next to mine."

"Hmm, the elderly man, right?"

Joni nodded. "Did you interview all the residents?"

"Yes."

"Did any of them see or hear anything?"

"I'm afraid not. Not that they're admitting to, anyway."

Joni rose to her feet and began to gather the dishes since everyone had finished eating.

"Leave them, love. I'll clean up." Tom reached for the dishes in her hand but she sidestepped and took them into the kitchen.

"I need to do something to show my appreciation for looking out for me, and then I am going to catch a bus into town, get some new clothes and go to work."

"I don't think that's—"

"No you're not," Gabe stated emphatically. "You've just had a scare and need to take it easy for a day or two."

"No."

"Damn it, Joni."

"No. I don't care what you say. I am going to work." Joni had already put the dishes on the counter and as she spoke she turned to face Gabe with her hands on her hips. There was no way in hell he was going to tell her she couldn't work.

"Fine, but if I see you are flagging, you'll be coming straight home."

Joni shrugged and turned her back on him. She wasn't going to be going home with him or his friends. Her car was still at the hotel and when she'd finished her shift she was going back to her own apartment to start cleaning up the mess. She didn't care that she would have to sleep on the floor. There was no way she was staying another night under their roof because she wasn't sure if she could keep her hands to herself.

It didn't matter that she liked being near them, liked being held by them, or touched and kissed by them. She needed to steer clear and that was exactly what she was going to do.

Chapter Eight

Gabe couldn't get Joni's answers to Gary's questions out of his head. Every time he'd asked her about family, friends or an ex-boyfriend who may have wrecked her place she'd negated it with an emphatic no. Did that mean she didn't have any living family? Did she have no friends or ex-boyfriends?

No she had friends, at least one, because she'd gone to the club to meet Kara. Maybe he should call and try to wrangle more information from her, but he didn't think she'd be any more cooperative now than she had been that night. He sighed with frustration as he filled another drink order.

It had been nearly two weeks since Joni had stayed the night at their house and even though he and his buddies had tried to convince her that she would be safer staying with them she'd held her ground.

He, Tom, and Gabe had taken turns driving by her place to make sure she was okay but there was nothing they could do unless she wanted them to. He was getting damn tired of her ignoring them. Oh, she was polite and answered when asked a question and spoke when necessary, but the distance between them felt so much more than it had been before.

He was in a constant state of arousal and no matter how many times he jacked off, it didn't help, and he knew he wouldn't be satiated until he had Joni underneath him and he was buried balls-deep in her hot, wet pussy.

At first he was a little disconcerted about how cool and distant she seemed but she couldn't hide her body language from them. They were experienced Doms and were trained to read every nuance of a person's actions. Joni was fighting them but also herself. She was fighting her attraction to them and that made him wonder if she'd had any experience with men at all. The more he watched the more he doubted she'd been with anyone and if she had, the fucker hadn't known the first thing about how to treat a woman.

"Hey," Gary said and sat on the barstool.

"Hi," Gabe replied and snagged a beer from the fridge before Gary asked for it.

"Thanks." Gary slugged half the bottle back before taking a breath.

"Rough day?" Gabe watched as Joni took a round of drinks out to a large group of men and although she smiled and laughed, not one ounce of humor touched her eyes.

"You could say that?"

"Want to talk about it?"

"Just got an escaped mental patient alert."

"Shit! How did that happen? What were they institutionalized for?"

"Murder."

"Fuck! How the hell did he escape?"

"One of the fucking staff left the delivery door unlocked. It was the patient's exercise time and they must have noticed the door hadn't clicked in. The only way he could have gotten out was in the back of one of those small freezer trucks."

"Don't they get searched before being let out?"

"No. A mental hospital's not like a prison."

"Maybe it should be."

"Yeah."

"And the person who left the door unlocked?"

"Fired."

"Just as well."

"There's a problem, Gabe." Gary scrubbed his hand over his face and then looked over his shoulder.

A knot of dread formed in Gabe's chest when he saw Gary was looking at Joni. When he turned back he motioned to Tom and Nic to come closer.

"What's going on?" Tom asked and listened as Gary quickly explained.

"So, I'm sure you've got every available cop out looking for this crazy," Nic said.

Gary nodded. "Don't let Joni go home."

Gabe straightened, clenched his teeth and fists, and waited for Gary's next words.

"The escaped patient is Joni's father."

"What?" Tom whispered and clutched the edge of the bar.

"Are you fucking kidding me?" Nic asked.

Gabe swallowed hard and drew in a deep breath. "Who'd he murder?"

"Her mother."

Gabe's ears started ringing and when he started seeing black spots realized he'd stopped breathing. All his dominant and protective instincts came roaring to life. There was no fucking way Joni was leaving his sight ever again. All this pussy footing around her because she was scared of her feelings was coming to an end. Right now! He wasn't letting her run anymore. He was going to make her face them head on and by the time he'd finished with her she was going to be screaming all of their names.

Once he had his emotions back under tight control he looked at Gary.

"Tell us all of it."

* * * *

Joni joked and laughed along with the group of guys she served but ever since she'd gone back home after spending the night in Gabe's, Nic's, and Tom's home, she'd felt hollow inside. It didn't seem to matter that she saw them every afternoon or night at work, nor that she spoke to them often.

There was a huge hole in her heart and she suspected it was because of them. It wasn't like the loss of her mother. It was totally different and she didn't know how to handle it. She glanced toward the bar and tensed when she saw Detective Gary Wade talking to all three of her employers.

That was another thing she couldn't understand. Why did they keep coming in to work when there was more than enough staff to cover the work hours?

Whatever Gary was telling them couldn't be good. Tom's face seemed to drain of color and then he was leaning on the edge of the bar. Nic looked like he was ready to punch someone and Gabe looked so tense and stood almost statue-still, she wondered if he was about to snap.

When she heard a whistle, she hurried over to the far table and began to collect some of the empty glasses littering the table. Normally, Joni would be working behind the bar but one of the casuals she'd hired had called in sick, so she was taking up the slack.

She couldn't believe how many people were now coming to the Three Comrades since Brent had added a little more sophistication to the specials menu. Even though she'd suggested that Tom, Nic, and Gabe didn't need to come in anymore they didn't listen and although she tried telling herself their presence had nothing to do with her, she was lying to herself. She sighed when she realized she'd just answered her earlier question to herself. Of course she knew why they hung around. She'd been lying to herself for the last couple of weeks and had almost made herself believe her own lies. She turned away from them and continued gathering dirty dishes.

After filling her tray with glasses she decided to put them in the kitchen dishwasher. The one behind the bar was fast but small, plus she wanted to avoid her employers as much as possible.

She'd emptied the clean dishes from it earlier and put them away, ready to be used for the quick wash cycle just in case. This was her third trip with a load full of dirty glasses and she figured two to three more and the machine would be full.

Joni closed the door after placing the last dirty glass in and nearly squealed when she slammed into a hard body when she turned. She'd been so intent on what she was doing and lost in thought she hadn't heard anyone follow her into the kitchen.

She took two steps back and bit her lip when she bumped into the counter and looked into Gabe's smoldering green eyes. He didn't give her a chance to speak or move and didn't say a word, but the next thing she knew she was in his arms and he was kissing her for all he was worth.

His mouth slanted over hers and his tongue pushed in to rub and dance with her own. Joni knew she should push him away, but she just couldn't find the energy to do it. Instead she moaned and clung to him as her legs turned to rubber and arousal exploded out from her core, setting all her nerve endings on fire. How long they kissed, she didn't know, nor care. All that mattered was he never stop.

When he finally broke the kiss she could only stare at him as she licked her lips and savored the taste of him on her tongue.

"This stops right now, Joni. We're not letting you run anymore, honey. You belong with and to us and we're not letting you deny it anymore."

Joni shook her head and sidestepped, all the while keeping her eyes on Gabe. She felt another presence beside her just before hands landed on her shoulders and turned her around.

She stared into Tom's hazel eyes unable to make herself look away and gasped when, as she watched his pupils dilate, his nostrils flared as he took a deep breath. "Gabe's right, love. You're ours."

Tom wrapped his arm around her waist and pulled her close and then he was kissing her. He tasted just as good as Gabe and Nic, but they all tasted different. Gabe was forceful and spicy, where Nic was zesty and convincing, but Tom was sweet and coaxing. It didn't seem to matter which of them kissed her, she couldn't stop herself from responding.

Each time one of them touched her, she found it harder and harder to ignore them and no matter how hard she tried to keep her desire for them under wraps it wasn't working.

And then she didn't want to anymore.

She was tired of fighting her feelings for them. Tired of keeping people at an arm's length. Tired of being alone, but if she opened herself up too much she would probably end up all alone once more.

Joni groaned and twirled her tongue around Tom's, savoring his wonderful taste on her buds and decided she would let whatever happened next, happen, but she would keep her heart out of the equation. There was no way she was setting herself up to be hurt ever again.

Tom slowed the voraciousness of the kiss down until he was sipping at her lips, until finally he lifted his mouth from hers. It didn't matter that her heart went all a flutter when any of them looked at her with desire. She was going to keep things on a physical level, and hopefully, when they walked away from her, her heart would still be intact.

* * * *

Nic watched Joni as they all pitched in to clean up. He could tell from the way she snuck glances at Tom and Gabe and the color rushing into her cheeks that something significant had happened. He'd seen his friends follow her into the kitchen, and when Joni rushed out after a good ten minutes had passed, her face was so pink she looked like she'd caught the sun.

She'd glanced over at him and caught him watching, so he'd smiled and winked at her trying to make her feel comfortable, but he wasn't sure he'd achieved that task when she looked away without responding and began collecting more dirty glasses.

She was currently on the far side of the room, wiping down tables and putting the cleaned chairs up so that when the cleaning staff came in all they needed to do was sweep, or vacuum and wash the tile floor.

"So, what happened?" He nodded toward Joni and then faced Tom and Gabe.

"We kissed," Tom said.

"Both of you?"

"Yeah." Gabe grinned and ran his fingers through his hair.

"And?" Nic waited because he knew there was more to tell.

"We told her she was ours and we weren't letting her run anymore," Tom answered.

Nic crossed his arms over his chest and raised an eyebrow in query. Although he probably looked cool, calm, and collected, he was far from it. His heart was beating so fast it felt like it was up in his throat, and even though he held his breath he wanted to gasp in lungfuls of air.

"She didn't say anything," Gabe explained.

"Shit!" Nic exhaled loudly and gripped the edge of the bar.

"But she didn't say no," Tom said.

"And her body language was acquiescent."

"That doesn't mean she agrees." Nic sighed with frustration and, when he saw movement from the corner of his eye and noticed Joni was walking toward them, he gave a slight shake of his head.

"All finished." Joni skirted the end of the bar and went to the small room off the other end where she placed the bucket and cleaning products. Nic wanted to grab her when she came back out and hoist her over his shoulder, rush her out to their truck, and take her home with them, but he needed to make sure she was on board with everything they wanted with her.

He moved to the side of the door and when she came out he reached out for her wrist and was thankful she didn't flinch. Little by little, over the last week or so, he and his friends had touched her often, getting her used to having them close and familiarizing her with their contact.

"Are you ready to come home with us, Joni?" Nic asked and once more found himself holding his breath. *God, I hate feeling so unsure around you, baby. Especially when I'm used to feeling confident, but I know you are the only woman who has ever meant so much to me, to us.*

Joni licked her lips nervously and glanced over to Gabe and Tom, before looking down at where his hand was looped gently around her wrist. He shifted his hold on her and caressed the soft sensitive skin of her inner wrist and watched as the pulse at the base of her neck leapt and beat rapidly. He glanced down at her shirt to see her hard nipples poking at the material and when he perused down farther, taking in her flared yet slim hips and her shapely legs, he nearly groaned when she shifted and pressed her thighs together.

Nic couldn't stand it another minute. He needed to feel her in his arms, to have her tongue in his mouth, her naked body beneath him as he surged his aching cock into her tight, wet cunt.

He released her wrist and waited for her to meet his gaze before snagging an arm around her waist and pulling her up against him.

"I want you, baby." Nic didn't give her a chance to reply. He quickly lowered his head and started kissing her hungrily. She responded without hesitation, moaning into his mouth as he pressed his tongue into and along hers. He drank her in and was ecstatic when she melted against him, her peaked nipples pressing into his chest making his hard cock twitch in his pants as it engorged to capacity.

When he felt her hips wiggle and her stomach press harder into his dick, he knew he had to stop before he picked her up, placed her on the bar, and took her right there. Their woman deserved a comfortable bed and silk sheets, because even though she was turning him on until he felt like he was on fire, he knew from her kisses and her unrestrained responses that she wasn't very experienced and that only made him want her more.

There was no pretentiousness in her, no feminine wiles. With Joni, what you saw was what you got, which he loved, but he also knew there was so much more to her that they had yet to discover. And if he had anything to say in the matter, he would know her from the inside out, very, very soon. But first he needed to hear the words from those sexy lips.

Nic slowed the kiss and finally lifted his head to look into her passion-hazed eyes. Her lips were red and swollen from his kisses and she looked a little dazed, as if she couldn't quite comprehend what was happening and that made him wonder if she was less experienced than he'd first thought. Made him wonder if she was actually untouched, but he wasn't about to ask her if she was a virgin since it could embarrass her and send her running.

"We all want to make love with you, Joni. Will you come home with us and let us show you how good it could be between us?"

Chapter Nine

The lust coursing through her body couldn't be denied. She'd spent the last couple of weeks trying to hide the way she felt whenever she was near Nic, Gabe, and Tom.

Yes, she could end up getting hurt, but she just couldn't make herself walk away. She'd managed to survive her ex after he beat the hell out of her, so surely this would be much easier to deal with once things fell apart, because she knew without a shadow of a doubt these three men would never harm her physically or intentionally.

Her self-confidence as an alluring, sexual woman had taken a pounding and because she felt safe with these men she wanted to know if she could have sex and actually feel something. Was she so distrustful that her heart was frozen without any hope of thawing?

There was only one way to find out.

Joni took a deep breath, licked her dry lips, and finally answered, "Yes."

Everything seemed to happen so fast after that, yet she felt like she moved in slow motion. She was ushered out the back door and found herself sitting in the passenger seat of her own car with Nic sitting beside her in the driver's seat. She couldn't even remember passing her keys over.

Nic must have seen how anxious she was, because he reached over, taking her hand in his, and glanced at her before looking back at the road. "Take a deep breath, baby. Everything is going to be fine. I promise."

"I don't know…" She paused because she wasn't sure how to put her roiling thoughts into words that would be comprehensible.

"Breathe with me, Joni," Nic said before taking a deep breath, holding it for a few seconds, and then exhaling. "Good. Again."

Joni inhaled and exhaled each time Nic did and found herself relaxing into her seat as her heart rate slowed.

"There you go," he said quietly and it took her a few moments to notice he was no longer driving and they were actually parked in the driveway of his and his friend's home. "Stay right there, baby. I'll come around and help you out."

Normally, she would have opened her own door, but her legs were feeling a bit weak and shaky, and she needed a little more time to get herself together. Her car door opened and before she could blink she was being led inside. She'd expected Nic to lead her straight to one of the bedrooms but he guided her into the kitchen where Gabe and Tom were already.

"Come and sit down, sweetheart." Gabe clasped her hand and tugged her over to the table where he pulled a chair out for her. Tom came over and placed a full wineglass on the table in front of her and Nic grabbed three bottles of beer and brought them over.

"We need to set up some rules, Joni." Tom sipped from his beer.

"Rules? What rules?"

"We want to do a scene with you," Gabe said.

"Um…"

"Just listen and if you have any questions at the end we will answer them. Okay?" Nic asked.

Joni nodded.

"You have all the tendencies of a submissive and we want to explore that with you," Tom said. "But never, ever think we will hurt you."

"There's a difference between being hit to erotic pain," Gabe began. "Having your bottom smacked brings all the blood to the surface and besides making your skin pink, which we all love, it can enhance pleasure exponentially."

"You will always have a safe word," Nic said. "If you are unsure and begin to get frightened we want you to say the word 'yellow.' We will pause with whatever we are doing and talk things over with you, but you will have to be open and honest with us. And believe me, we will definitely know if you are lying. We've all had a hell of a lot of experience reading body language and can see a lie from a mile away."

"Can you do that, Joni?" Tom asked. "Can you open yourself up to us?"

Joni's first instinct was to nod but she wasn't really sure that was true. "I don't know."

Gabe shoved his chair back, rose to his feet, and walked around to her side of the table. He pulled her seat back and then scooped her up before sitting where she'd been and plonked her ass on his lap. He tugged on her braid, tilting her head back, and smiled down at her.

"Thank you for answering truthfully." Gabe lowered his head and kissed her lightly on the lips. "I think that's the first time you've ever been totally honest with us."

Joni's heart filled with warmth. She couldn't believe that a little bit of praise made her feel so good and wanted more of it.

"You like being praised, don't you, baby?" Nic asked, but the smile on his face let her know he already knew the answer, so she nodded.

"Good." Tom clasped her hand. "In BDSM it is a Dominant's job to free his sub from all the constrictions she places on herself."

"What do you mean?" Joni took a sip of wine and sighed as the moisture coated her dry mouth and throat.

"You may think you can't handle something, but it's a Dom's job to push a sub's boundaries," Nic explained.

"I don't—"

"Wait until we're finished," Gabe said.

She nodded again.

"We will always have our woman's best interests at heart. In no way would we ever hurt or push beyond what you can handle." Tom squeezed her hand.

"You can use your safe word if you are scared or if we do something you don't like," Nic said.

"What word will you use if you're unsure and need to talk or just have a bit of a break?" Gabe asked.

"Yellow."

"Good girl." Tom smiled.

"And what word will you use if you want everything to stop?" Nic asked.

"Red."

"That's right," Gabe said. "There are times when a Dom will ask his sub where she's at throughout a scene. Most Doms and clubs like to keep things uncomplicated and use the traffic light system. So if we ask how you're feeling and you're comfortable with what we're doing you will answer with 'green.' Do you understand, Joni?"

"Yes."

"Right." Nic rubbed his hands together as if he were eager to get started but he stayed in his seat. "Do you know how to address a Dom?"

"Uh…" Joni nibbled on her lip as she tried to remember how Kara had addressed her men. "Sir?"

"Yes." Tom smiled at her again. "And maybe when you're more comfortable you can address us as master, but we need to gain your trust first. Don't we, honey?"

Joni felt a little awkward about answering that question, but from the way they were all watching her so intently, she knew they were waiting for her to lie. She pushed her chin up and answered honestly. "Yes."

Gabe ran a hand up and down her back causing goose bumps to break out over her skin and she couldn't stop from shivering as she met his intent blue eyes. "I'm proud of you, Joni. I know your first instinct was to lie."

She blinked as more warmth filled her heart at his praise and then he wrapped her braid around his wrist and pulled her mouth toward his. And then she was drowning.

Drowning in his heat, his taste, his masculinity, and his passion and she couldn't get enough. She felt him release her hair and then his arms were around her body and he was moving, but she was so lost in his kisses, her eyelids heavy with lust, she couldn't open them to see where he was taking her. Not that she really cared right then. All that mattered was that she taste everything he had to give her.

She was so hungry for him, for them all, that her clothes were an abrasive restriction she couldn't wait to get rid of. Her skin, her whole body, felt achy and she wanted their hands on her, taking the pleasurable pain away. Joni whimpered in protest when her feet were lowered to the floor and Gabe broke the kiss. Her breath caught and her heart stuttered in her throat when she opened her eyes. She blinked a couple of times just to make sure she wasn't seeing things and, when she realized she wasn't dreaming, her pussy clenched and cream dripped onto her already soaked undies.

"When we are in this room you are not to speak unless we ask you a question and when we do we expect an immediate answer. Is that understood?" Nic asked in a stern voice.

"Yes."

"Yes what?" Gabe almost barked the question out.

"Yes, sir," she whispered.

"Say it again but this time louder," Nic demanded.

"Yes, sir."

"Good girl," Tom praised from behind her. "We control everything in this room. We control your body, your passion, and your orgasms. You don't get to come unless we tell you to. Okay?"

"Yes, sir."

"It's getting easier, isn't it, love?" Tom asked.

Joni didn't pretend she didn't know what he was talking about because she did. Each time she replied with "yes sir" the words came easier to her lips until it felt natural.

"Yes, sir."

"Strip, Joni," Gabe ordered.

Heat filled her cheeks and, although she wasn't comfortable about being naked in front of anyone, when she glanced up from beneath her eyelashes and saw Nic and Gabe looking at her with lust, she reached for the buttons on her shirt.

She didn't hurry but by the time she was standing in front of them totally bare she was shaking in reaction. She rolled her shoulders forward and moved her arms in front of her, trying to hide her breasts and pussy at the same time.

"Stop," Nic said. "Put your arms back by your sides."

Joni complied and lowered her head. She didn't want to see them when they found all the flaws she saw when she looked at herself in the mirror. She didn't think she could stand it if she saw revulsion on their faces when they noticed the stretch marks on the outside of her upper thighs or hips. She wasn't that tall but when she'd hit puberty she had seemed to grow almost overnight and her skin had stretched and marked and no matter what she'd tried in oils and lotions, nothing had been able to diminish the rapid growth scars.

John had often taunted her about how ugly those blemishes were and she had been self-conscious of them ever since.

"So fucking sexy," Tom whispered, his breath against her ear making her shiver. He moved closer and she could feel the heat of his body on her back. When his hands landed on her hips and then skimmed down the outside of her thighs to her knees and back again, she tensed and waited for the disparaging remarks.

"What was that thought, Joni?" Tom asked.

"Wh... Sorry, sir?"

"What went through your mind when Tom's hands caressed over your hips and legs?" Gabe asked in a firm voice.

Joni shook her head, looking down at the floor, and hoped they couldn't see how red her face felt or how ashamed she was.

"Let's get her on the spanking bench," Nic ordered.

Joni wanted to protest but remembered she wasn't supposed to speak unless she was asked a question. And when she was scooped off her feet and into Tom's arms and carried over to the padded bench. He lowered her to her feet, placed his hands on her hips, and turned her until she was facing the bench.

"On your knees, love." Tom applied pressure to her shoulders and she slowly knelt down. "Lean over the bench with your breasts on the outside of the pad."

Joni bent and carefully adjusted her breasts so that they weren't squished against the edge of the pads, until the cushion was between them.

"Give me your hands," Tom ordered and she did. He clasped her wrist and her breathing escalated when she felt soft cuffs wrap around her and he secured her arms so she couldn't move. Sweat formed on her brow when another hand ran up her calf and then a strap was crossed over her upper thigh. The process was repeated until she could only move her body and not her limbs.

Her breaths were panting in and out at a rapid pace and her heart was beating so fast it hurt.

Hands landed on her back, caressing up and down in a smoothing motion. "Are we hurting you, Joni?" Gabe asked.

"No, sir."

"Are you in any pain?" Nic asked.

"No, sir."

"Are you scared of being tied up?" Tom asked.

"No, sir."

"Are you scared of being hurt?" Gabe questioned.

Joni licked her lips and then flinched when a hand landed on her ass. It wasn't a hard hit, but it was enough to warm her skin.

"Did that hurt, Joni?" Nic moved around and squatted down in front of her so she could see his face.

"No, sir."

"Are you scared of getting hurt, sub?" Gabe asked.

"Yes, sir."

"Good girl," Nic praised and then he kissed her. His tongue pressed in, swirled around, and then he drew away again.

"Honesty gets rewarded," Gabe said.

Joni's eyes closed and she moaned when a finger ran up through her wet folds, circled her clit a few times, and then caressed back down to dip into her creamy cunt.

"So fucking wet," Gabe said in a growly voice.

"Have you had sex before, Joni?" Nic asked.

"Yes, sir."

"And was it good sex?" Tom asked.

Joni wished he'd move away from her so she could answer without being watched but she had a feeling even if they were all standing behind her and she lied they would know. She felt like she couldn't hide anything from these men and her soul was right there for them to read, but she wasn't about to let go totally. She just wanted to have sex with them and when they were tired of her, she would leave with her head held high, but she had a feeling she had bitten off way more than she could chew.

When she'd agreed to come home with them she'd expected to be taken to the bedroom, fucked, and then she would leave again. She hadn't forgotten they were Doms or where she'd met them, but had assumed that because they weren't going to that BDSM club that their dominant tendencies would be put on the backburner. Boy had she been wrong.

She knew she could have left without seeing any of this through but there was something about them that drew her to them. Maybe it was their confidence. That was definitely a turn-on, but she had a feeling it was so much more than that. Yes they were all good-looking, sexy men with muscular physiques that would draw the eye of any woman, but there was this caring visage about them she just couldn't walk away from.

And if that made her a fool, then so be it.

Chapter Ten

Joni's hesitation was answer enough but Gabe wasn't about to let her get away with any infractions. She needed to learn what they liked when they were playing in a scene or in the bedroom, so he raised his hand and smacked her ass. He didn't smack her hard but it was enough to sting and let her know he and his friends meant business.

Gabe had a feeling this night was the night that would make or break their chance with their little sub and although he knew she could take much more than he was dishing out, he wanted to start off slow and get her used to what they needed. Plus this was the first time she'd dealt with being a sub and they needed to gain her trust. If that meant holding back at the start, until she was comfortable and begged for more, then that was what they'd do.

He was so fucking hard he wanted to pull his cock from his pants, kneel behind her, and shove into her until he was balls-deep, but they needed to know more so they could handle any issues she may have. And he knew there were issues.

"Answer Tom, now, sub!" Gabe demanded, bringing his hand down on her ass once more, but this time adding a little more force behind his hand. She moaned and her back arched and he knew right then and there that she was abso-fucking-lutely perfect for them.

"No!"

"No, what?" Nic asked.

"No the sex wasn't good...sir."

"Do you know why?" Gabe asked.

"Because of me," Joni sobbed.

"What the hell?" Tom spat before taking her cheeks between his hands and lifting her head until she was looking at him.

"Who the fuck told you that?" Gabe was so angry he nearly roared his question but drew in a deep steadying breath when Tom glanced at him and shook his head slightly.

"It wasn't your fault, honey," Tom said quietly before leaning in and kissing her on the forehead. "Whoever he was lied to cover up for his own inadequacies."

"You can't say that. You didn't even know him."

"Untie her," Tom said as he started to unbind her wrists and even though Gabe wanted to show her the world of BDSM, she needed to be shown what true loving and caring was first.

With Nic's help, they undid the straps around her thighs and then he lifted her up into his arms and carried her across to the sofa on the other side of the room where he sat, taking her with him.

"Let me guess," Gabe said as he adjusted her on his lap and held her snuggly in his arms. "This ex started picking on your clothes, the way you did your hair and your body, and when it came to sex, he didn't take the time to make sure you were ready for him and hurt you while he took his own pleasure."

When he heard Joni sniffle he knew he'd hit the proverbial nail on the head. Anger raced through his body, pumping his muscles up, and he clenched his jaw so he wouldn't shout with ire.

"Joni, look at me," Nic demanded as he scooted off the sofa and knelt in front of her. "Oh, baby, don't cry."

"You have nothing to be ashamed or embarrassed over, sweetheart. You ex was the defective one. Not you." Gabe kissed the top of her head.

"He was married," Joni spoke so quietly.

"He lied to you, didn't he?" Nic asked.

Although Gabe awaited her answer, he didn't need to hear her reply, because he already knew what her answer would be.

"Yes."

"Tell us what happened, honey." Tom stroked a hand over her head.

"It was nearly two years ago now."

"Time has nothing to do with how that asshole hurt you." Nic lifted her hand to his mouth and kissed the back of it. "You need to tell us what happened, Joni. If you don't get that pain festering inside you out, you're never going to be able to move forward."

Joni nodded in agreement but Gabe knew she struggled with opening up with them. He wanted to give her a little verbal nudge but decided to wait and see if she would begin talking on her own merit.

"I was at a really vulnerable stage in my life," Joni began.

Gabe wanted to ask her about that but decided to wait and see if she would explain. "My mom had just died and I was still grieving. I met John when he came into the restaurant and he must have been attracted to me because he came back almost every Friday.

"I was flattered with the compliments and the flirting because no one had ever paid attention to me like that before."

"How long did it take him to wear you down and date him?" Tom asked.

"Three months."

"And in those three months he was attentive, giving you compliments, and swept you off of your feet," Nic said.

"Yes."

"Did you move in with him?" Gabe asked.

"He...moved in with me."

"He played you, baby." Nic rubbed a hand up and down her thigh in a comforting caress.

"That may be so, but if I hadn't been so naïve, he would never have been able to fool me."

"How did you find out about his wife?" Tom asked.

Joni sucked in a noisy breath and exhaled raggedly. "He'd been drinking and he was picking at everything I did. The food I cooked wasn't tasty enough, his clothes weren't washed and ready for him to pack the next morning. You name it he denigrated everything I did.

"It was then I realized that I would never be good enough in his eyes. I was sick and tired of listening to his complaining and disparaging comments, so I stormed from the kitchen, grabbing his things as I went, and shoved them into his bag and garbage bags. He didn't even bother moving from his seat to see what I was doing. He was too busy drinking.

"When I was done I opened the front door and threw his things outside and went back to face him."

Gabe tightened his hold on her when he felt her shiver, but when her trembling didn't stop and only got stronger he feared what she would say next.

"I told him to get out and never come back. He'd had this supercilious look in his eyes when he looked at me and complained but that disdainful look was wiped from his face and changed to one of pure hatred. I was scared but I wasn't about to let him know he was intimidating me and held my ground when he got up and walked toward me." Joni sobbed but even though tears didn't form in her eyes, Gabe knew she was holding on by a thread.

"I should have run. He hit me in the jaw first and I went flying across the room and I was stunned, barely able to see and I think I was in shock. He rushed over and hit me over and over again. I have no idea how long for but I must have screamed or cried out because I heard banging but thought it was him hitting the wall in his rage. I don't know when he left or how long he'd been gone but it couldn't have been long. One of my neighbors broke into my apartment and when he found me called the paramedics and the police."

"Fuck!" Nic shot to his feet, spun away, and began to pace.

"What were your injuries, Joni?" Tom asked in a hoarse voice.

"I was bruised and swollen, two fractured ribs and a broken wrist."

"Motherfucking bastard," Gabe snarled with anger, unable to hold his rage in at what had been done to his woman. When he realized she was cold and trembling even more, he motioned to Nic to bring him a blanket and quickly wrapped it around her body.

"Did you report him to the police?" Nic clenched his fists as he squatted down in front of him and Joni again.

"Yes, but they couldn't find any record of one John Vander having ever been born."

"So how did they find him?" Tom held her hand between his as if trying to warm it.

"I remembered his license plate. Turns out his real name was Angus Peace and he was married with three kids."

"Damn, baby, he lied to you. Don't feel guilty for his sins." Nic frowned as he took in her quaking body.

"Yeah try telling that to his wife and children." Joni covered her mouth but still couldn't contain her sob of pain.

"She came to see me, asking me to drop the charges."

"Geezus," Tom muttered.

"I couldn't. I felt so sorry for her, but if he'd done this to me what's to say he hadn't and wouldn't do it to another unsuspecting woman. His wife had this look in her eyes and I knew he'd hurt her, too. But I couldn't let him get away with what he'd done and even though I'd never met them or knew how old they were, I feared for his kids, too.

"Someone like that never changes his spots and there was no way in hell I was letting him hurt innocent children."

"Good for you, sweetheart." Gabe kissed her on the head. "You were so strong and brave."

Joni shook her head. "No, I wasn't. If I had been I would have ended it a lot sooner than I did. And do you know what the worst part about that was?"

Gabe didn't want to ask because he had a feeling he wasn't going to like the answer one little bit, but he couldn't, not when he felt the tension in her body as she awaited his question. He braced himself for the fury he knew he was going to feel but made sure to keep his grip on her gentle so he wouldn't hurt her.

"What?"

"That fucker only got a six-week suspended sentence because it was his first charge. One good thing did come of it though. His wife came back and actually thanked me for pressing charges. There was this relief in her eyes and I think that because I wouldn't back down it gave her the courage to make a stand, too.

"She told me she was filing for a divorce, going home to pack her kids up, and leave. And although I was glad she had finally found the courage to do so, I still carry the guilt of breaking up her marriage. Those kids need both parents and because of me they only have their mother."

Motherfucking asshole. Fucking shit. Fuck! Fuck! Fuck!

"No, sweetheart, because of you they have a healthy mother. That bastard probably would have ended up escalating and may well have ended up killing her. What would have happened to those kids if he'd murdered his own wife and been sent to prison for years? They may not have ended up with anyone to care for them. They probably would have ended up in the system and that would have been a travesty.

"Because of you, they still have a mother to love them. The marriage break-up didn't have anything to do with you. Everything that happened was all on him, Joni. Never you, sweetheart."

Gabe felt moisture plop on his arm, and realized this was probably the first time she'd ever cried over what had happened. He pulled her more firmly into his body and held her as the storm raged inside of her. But for some reason he had a feeling she cried for more than the betrayal from her ex. The wealth of tears were so many he was worried she would make herself ill.

Finally she cried herself out and when he felt her body go lax against his, he knew that she slept.

Although they had stopped the scene before it had really started, because Joni had begun to open up and share some to the pain she'd held within, Gabe knew that he, Nic, and Tom had more work to do. And not just the BDSM aspect.

Yes, she was beginning to trust them but she was still holding back and until she let herself go and gave up that hard-worn control, the walls around her emotions and her heart, she was a flight danger.

"She's asleep." Nic stood up and began to pace.

"Get onto Gary and see if he can find out where that fucker is," Gabe demanded in a quiet voice. How he was able to keep his voice so low was beyond him, because inside he was a raging tumultuous storm with no outlet.

"On it," Tom said and then headed out of the room pulling his cell from his pocket as he went.

"You think this bastard is the one who trashed her place?"

"It's a possibility. Don't you think?"

"Yeah. Not unless one of the people she worked at that restaurant with had it in for her," Nic suggested.

"I'd thought of that but when we called her previous employer, he had nothing but praise for her."

"That doesn't mean everyone working there agreed with the boss's opinion. For all we know she could have stepped on someone's toes when she was hired."

"Look into it." Gabe rose to his feet, cradling Joni against his chest.

"What about the other residents of the apartment building?"

Gabe nodded. He hated that Joni was in danger and wasn't about to overlook any suggestion when it came to her safety. What he hated most, though, was having nothing to go on. If Joni had no idea who had it in for her, they were searching blind, and he didn't like that at all.

There was only one way to keep her safe and he wasn't going to take no for an answer.

Joni was moving back in with them. No ifs, no buts, no maybes. She didn't have a say in the matter.

* * * *

Joni woke feeling like she'd been hit by a truck emotionally. She was a little embarrassed she had fallen apart so quickly and easily. And although she had told Gabe, Nic, and Tom about Angus and what he'd done to her, she hadn't been able to tell them about what her father had done to her mother.

It didn't seem to matter that it had been years since that bastard had murdered her mom, the pain inside was still so raw, she didn't think she'd ever be able to speak about it. Not even Kara knew how her mother had died. Just the thought of saying the words made her feel physically ill.

She shifted and tensed when she felt a large warm body right up against her own. When she inhaled she knew from the sandalwood scent that it was Nic in bed with her. She blinked and saw from the light seeping in around the blinds on the window that it was quite late in the morning.

"How are you feeling, baby?" The rumble of Nic's deep voice sent shivers racing up and down her spine and when she felt her areolae contract and pucker she realized she was totally naked. She moved her legs and nearly sighed with pleasure when Nic's bare, lightly hairy legs brushed against hers.

"I'm okay."

"Did you sleep well?"

She nodded and relished the sensation of her cheek against his skin. Her head was resting in the crook of her shoulder and chest and his front was plastered to her back. "Yes, thanks."

"Hmm." Nic inhaled deeply and nibbled on her neck. "You smell so good, baby."

Joni wanted to turn over but wasn't sure what to say or do so she remained still. His lips trailed down her neck and then nibbled on her collarbone when he shifted and leaned over her.

"Your skin is so warm and soft." The hand on her belly moved and caressed over her flesh, smoothing from her hip, dipping in at her waist, and stopping on the outside of her breast.

Her breath hitched in her throat as she waited for him to touch her where she ached to be touched, but when he didn't move, she groaned with frustration.

"Are you aching, baby?" His warm breath sent a shiver ripping through her body. "Do you want my hands on you? Do you want me to make love with you?"

"Yes," Joni moaned before she could bite back the words. "Please?"

Nic shifted away and Joni had to bite her lip to hold in her protest, but then she was rolled over onto her back with him leaning over her and staring intently into her eyes. His brown eyes were so full of lust she reached up and cupped his cheek, wanting to pull him down so she could kiss him.

"If we do this, Joni. There will be no going back."

"What?" She knew what he'd said, but wasn't sure she understood what he meant.

"If I make love to you then you will belong to Gabe, Tom, and I. There will be no more holding back."

"I'm not—"

"Shh." Nic placed a finger over her lips, effectively silencing her. "You are. We know how to read you, baby. You may have told us about that asshole, but you're still holding out on us. If you let me love you, you will belong to us from now on. You will need to obey our demands of you in the bedroom and when we are scening with you. If you don't then we will punish you."

Joni didn't care about anything right now except having Nic take away the interminable ache she'd been living with since the first time she'd seen all of them at the club. And if everything went to pot afterward, then she'd have to deal with the consequences but she couldn't walk away. She needed him, needed all of them more than she'd needed anything else in her life.

Ever.

Chapter Eleven

Nic waited with bated breath for Joni's answer. When she looked him in the eye he didn't need her verbal affirmation to know what her reply was going to be. He could see it in her eyes, but he still wanted, needed, to hear her voice affirming her body language.

She reached up and cupped his cheek and although he wanted to rub his skin on hers, he held completely still. And then the soft whisper of her voice filled him with elation.

"Yes."

Thank you, God.

Nic didn't waste any time. He shifted her more fully onto her back and then moved over the top of her and wished he didn't still have his boxers on. His cock was so damn hard it was throbbing along with each beat of his heart.

He lowered his head and was pleased when her eyes slowly closed and then he was kissing her. He normally would have gone slowly, but he was so hungry for her he couldn't stop himself from devouring her. His tongue pushed into her mouth, rubbing along and swirling around with hers in the beginning of a passionate dance. He lifted to his elbows and skimmed his hands over her surprisingly large breasts. She was quite a petite woman and, though she was in proportion, her breasts were bigger than a handful.

When his hands made contact with her rib cage she whimpered and the closer he got to those magnificent tits, the louder her noises of passion became. He finally cupped them in his hands, savoring the weight of them as he kneaded and molded them with his fingers and palms.

He thrummed the taut, rosy peaks with his thumbs and her mewls became more guttural and sounded a little surprised as if she'd never gained pleasure from having her nipples touched. That only made him more determined to make sure everything he did with her elicited more of her desire. When his lungs began burning he broke the kiss, gasped in a breath, and moved his way down her neck, licking, kissing and nibbling, taking note of each erogenous zone before continuing on.

Licking around the outside of one breast, he smiled when she arched her chest up toward him, silently begging for more. When he felt a caress of air at his back he knew that Tom and Gabe had entered the room, but ignored them as he finally laved his tongue over the taut berry and then sucked it deeply into his mouth.

She cried out and gasped with need and then he moved onto her other nipple, giving it the same attention he gave the first. When she writhed beneath him, her legs moving restlessly, he shifted down her body, stopping to suck on the soft yet toned skin of her lower abdomen, before licking around her belly button.

Nic maneuvered between her legs, using his shoulders to spread her legs wider and he inhaled deeply, taking the sweet musky scent of her arousal into his nose and lungs as he stared at the trimmed strip of hair on the top of her mound. Her bare, plump pussy lips glistened with her creamy dew.

After wrapping his arms around her upper thighs he spread her wider and lowered his head, taking a long slow swipe with his tongue through her juicy folds, relishing the flavor of her cream on his taste buds.

She cried out when the tip of his tongue flicked over her engorged clit and he opened his eyes to watch her as he took another lick. Tom and Gabe had stripped down to their underwear and were in the process of getting on the bed either side of her, but she was so caught up in the pleasurable sensations he was bestowing on her, she didn't seem to notice.

Nic's cock pulsed and a drop of pre-cum dribbled from the slit, coating the head of his dick, and making him so ravenous for her. He wanted to crawl back up over her and sink into her heat right then, but first he needed to show her how good he could make her feel.

He levered up onto an elbow, still with his arms wrapped around her thighs and as he lapped at her clit, he penetrated her dripping wet cunt with a finger. She gasped and moaned and when he felt her hands in his hair, he met Gabe's eyes and nodded at him.

Gabe nudged Tom and then they each took a wrist in one of their large hands, lifted them above her head, and pinned them to the mattress.

"Oh, god," she gasped out between panting breaths before she was silenced with Gabe's mouth on hers.

Nic began to stroke his finger in and out of her juicy hole, making sure to lick her in sync with his pumping digit. Each time he pressed back in, he ramped up the speed and depth of his penetration, as well as his lapping tongue. When the muscles in her legs began to shake and became tenser, he knew she was climbing the peak to ecstasy. Her muffled cries were music to his ears and he glanced up as Tom bent to suckle on one of her nipples, while Gabe began pinching and plucking on the other one.

Her arousal was so high, her pussy leaked copious amounts of juices, coating his fingers and hand, and he added another finger. He and his friends were big men all over and he needed to make sure she was stretched out so they wouldn't hurt her when they made love to her.

By the time he added a third finger Joni was so tense it was like rigor mortis had set in and then she was screaming. He rubbed the pads of his fingers over her G-spot and then spread his fingers as he sucked on her clit.

Her whole body jerked as her internal muscles pulsed and contracted with her orgasm. He never let up with his stroking fingers or lapping tongue as she came and when she gushed with ejaculate he growled with pleasure and drank down her cream.

Nic eased his digits from her still-twitching cunt, licked them clean, and then grabbed the condom Gabe handed him, before suiting up. He just hoped that he could contain his passion and make her come again before he shot his load, but he was a Dom and wasn't about to concede to his carnal urges. Well he was, but not before making sure Joni climaxed again.

* * * *

Joni was still gasping for breath and trying to wrap her head around the explosive orgasm she'd just had. She'd never experienced anything like that in her life and although the edge had been taken off, she wanted more. So much more.

Her eyes fluttered open to meet Nic's hungry gaze just before Gabe leaned down to suck on one of her nipples. Tom released her other peak with a loud *pop* and then his mouth was on hers. Her whole body was one big massive ache and she knew only these three men could diminish the low burn smoldering inside.

She whimpered when Nic rubbed the tip of his condom-covered dick through her drenched folds and then moaned when the head of his cock pressed on her clit.

"You have got to be the sexiest woman I have ever seen," Nic said in a deep raspy voice.

Joni didn't think she was anything special but she wasn't about to refute the way he saw her. Plus, the compliment sent a wave of warmth into her chest and heart before the fire sprang up a little more.

"Are you ready for me, baby?" he asked as he moved the tip of his cock down to kiss against her entrance.

Her pussy clenched as if trying to pull him in. When she tried to reach for him to let him know she wanted him just as much as he seemed to want her, she found her arms still pressed into the mattress by the hold Tom and Gabe had on her. She quivered with excitement.

"Yes," she groaned.

And then she held her breath as the head of Nic's hard, hot cock pressed into her, stretching her delicate tissues, eliciting a pleasurable burn to travel deep into her core.

"You're so fucking hot. Wet. Tight," Nic groaned as he pressed in farther.

"More," Joni begged, needing him to press in to appease the deep ache and then he was looking at her with a frown as he stopped.

"You don't get to control what happens in the bedroom, Joni. You are ours to pleasure and command. Do you understand?" he asked in a cool voice, but the heat in his eyes belied his impartiality.

"Yes…sir," she tacked on the last word after a pause and her breath hitched in her throat when the frown was replaced by a smile.

"Such a good little sub." He rewarded her by withdrawing a bit before sinking farther into her pussy. "I think Gabe has something for you, baby."

Joni turned her head to see that Gabe had removed his boxers and was now lying on his side, sort of curved around her head with his hand pumping up and down his long, thick shaft. She licked her lips when she saw the bead of clear moisture on the tip of his dick and wondered what it tasted like. She blinked when she realized her arms had been moved down and crossed over her torso just beneath her breasts. She'd been so caught up in the sensation of Nic's rod pushing into her she hadn't noticed anything else.

Tom had a hand on top of her crossed wrists, holding her arms in place, and she loved it. Loved that she didn't have to worry about whether to touch them or not. Her choice had been taken away and it was an enlightening and desire-heightening experience.

"Joni, look at me," Gabe demanded as he gripped her chin and turned her head back to him. "I need to feel your mouth on my cock, sweetheart. Open up."

Joni quickly licked her dry lips as Gabe shifted closer. The tip of her tongue ended up making contact with the head of his cock and she moaned at the sweet-spicy flavor exploding on her buds. She opened her mouth wide and was about to lean forward to take the head of his cock into her mouth, but he canted his hips, pressing it in.

She closed her eyes, hollowed her cheeks, and opened her mouth as wide as she could, but remained still, allowing him to dictate how much she would take.

"Fucking beautiful," Gabe said in a growly voice. "So much fucking trust."

That was when Joni realized she was way more trusting of Gabe, Nic, and Tom than she'd ever been with anyone else, including Kara. If she hadn't trusted them, she would be shaking in her boots about letting them control her. Her pussy clenched and she mewled as Gabe began to gently rock his hips, gliding his cock in and out of her mouth, going a little deeper with each press forward.

Nic was all the way inside of her and she could feel the corona of his cock pressing against her womb, but instead of hurting and turning her off, it only heightened her awareness and arousal. She pushed her hips up from the bed, trying to get him to move, but ended up squealing when he slapped her pussy. The burn on her clit sent shooting sparks of blissful electricity deep into her womb, making her clench around his wide cock.

"Oh, shit, yeah," Nic rasped. "You like getting your pussy spanked don't you, baby?"

Since she couldn't answer with her mouth full of cock she hummed instead and then she moaned when Tom sucked on a nipple.

She was so overwhelmed but not in a bad way. She was incredulous at having three ruggedly handsome, sexy, muscular, manly men making love to her. Each time Tom sucked her nipple she matched her suctioning on Gabe's cock to his rhythm. She wanted to demand that Nic move, but knew to stay silent and still.

The dominance they were governing her with only made her crave more and even though she was used to guarding herself around others, she felt the restrictions she'd placed on herself slowly seeping away.

"That's it, sweetheart." Gabe stroked her cheek as he pressed in deeper before withdrawing to the tip. "Let it all go."

Joni blinked when moisture burned the back of her eyes but she didn't let the tears form. She couldn't believe how light and free she felt at not having to control everything around her, including herself. She would have to revisit and think over those feelings later, but for now she just wanted to feel.

Nic was moving again, his hips rocking forward and back, sliding his cock in a slow gentle rhythm, but each time he drove forward again he increased the pace and depth until his flesh was slapping against hers. Gabe swayed faster, his cock gliding along her tongue and she made sure to caress it along the underside of his dick. He must have liked that because each time she did it he moaned.

Tom alternated from nipple to nipple, sucking and biting it one minute, and then pinching and plucking at it the next.

The ache inside of her was now a manifesting burn, getting hotter and brighter until she was so tense with wanting, she was sure she was about to break.

Nic was now fucking her hard, fast, and deep, the pleasure so intense she was sure she would shatter. Her pussy walls began to contract and she sucked harder and faster on Gabe's cock.

Liquid heat raced through her veins, making her feel totally boneless, yet at the same time she was as tense as a coil. And then everything seemed to happen at once.

Tom bit one of her nipples at the same time he pinched the other one hard. Gabe's cock jerked in her mouth and he shouted before nudging the back of her throat as he came and her pussy clamped down so hard she saw stars.

She swallowed reflexively drinking down Gabe's cum, savoring his spicy flavor as her cunt quivered and quaked, covering Nic's prophylactic-covered cock in her juices as he pounded in and out of her. She would have screamed if she were able, but as she continued to swallow she saw stars and an emotion unlike anything she'd ever felt before invaded her heart.

The nirvana washing over her was so much, yet it was nothing compared to the way her heart filled with love.

She heard Nic roar and then he shoved forward, pressing and holding his cock deep in her contracting cunt as he came. Joni felt like she'd been pulled apart into a million little pieces, but when she was put back together, the walls encasing her emotions and heart had been left out.

It wasn't until Gabe removed his softening cock from her mouth that she realized she was trembling so hard in reaction, and although she pressed her lips together, her teeth were chattering. Even opening her mouth again as she panted for air didn't stop the quaking of her teeth, jaw, or body.

Nic eased his cock from her pussy and then she was lifted from the bed up into Gabe's arms.

Her wet cheeks connected with his bare chest and, although she swallowed and tried to hold in her emotions, she began sobbing. Warmth pressed into her back and sides and she was surrounded by three large men.

Tom and Nic ran soothing hands up and down her body while Gabe held her tight, rocking her gently to and fro as if she were a small child.

It took her a while to comprehend what they were saying and although she felt like an idiot for breaking down, she was relieved they couldn't read her mind.

"We knew you had a lot of passion hidden inside you, sweetheart." Gabe kissed the top of her head.

"Thank you for trusting us, baby." Nic rubbed her back.

"You have so much locked away, love. Thank you for agreeing to be with us and entrusting your care to us." Tom kissed her shoulder.

Finally, her tears slowed and even though she felt a little foolish, Joni felt so much better. The crying had been cathartic and that was when she realized maybe she was submissive after all, and that these Doms could help to set her free.

* * * *

Paul was so angry he could have committed murder. He'd followed her and those three assholes back to their house and waited for the lights to be turned off to case the joint. When he'd seen the security system he knew he couldn't get to Joni here, but he wasn't about to give up.

He'd followed her to her new place of work and staked out the back for hour upon hour, but she never came out alone. One of those fuckers always walked her to her car. When he'd seen the cleaning company arrive just after everyone left a plan began to form in his mind. He took down the number on the side of the cleaning van and decided to apply for another job. It wouldn't hurt to earn a few extra bucks cleaning while he was on vacation.

First thing tomorrow he was going to call that company and get work at the Three Comrades Hotel.

Joni deserved to be punished for ignoring him. She should be in his bed, not fucking those assholes.

He would bide his time and plan, but in the end she would be his.

Chapter Twelve

Tom had been watching Joni intently the whole time Nic had made love to her and she'd been sucking Gabe off. The moment her climax had been upon her was the moment he'd seen vulnerable bewilderment in her eyes. And then they filled with so much emotion as she'd come down from her climactic high, she'd broken.

Not broken in spirit but in the containment of her feelings and passions. Now that they were getting to the true woman she'd hidden away from the world and even from herself, he knew things were going to be okay.

He'd known from the first moment he'd spied her on the monitor that she was special and, although he couldn't wait to make love with her and show her with his body how much she meant to him, he wasn't sure she was up to another round of lovemaking.

But then she surprised him. She wiped the tears from her face, kissed Gabe and then Nic on the lips, and then turned and crawled up onto his lap. She wrapped her arms around his waist and hugged him tightly before drawing back to meet his gaze.

The desire he saw in her eyes rekindled his own and before he stopped to think about what he was doing, he was kissing her voraciously. She matched him lick for lick, swirling her tongue with his until he was desperate to be inside of her.

Tom broke the kiss, lifted her onto her hands and knees, and moved in behind her. He slapped her ass and smiled when she moaned before pushing back against him, begging for more. He knew he shouldn't let her move, but he was so happy she was with them. She was the sub they had been waiting for and he didn't take her to task right now. He did slap her other ass cheek though and then he smoothed his hands over the warm pink skin, which elicited a whimper of need from her, before he wrapped an arm around her hips and reached down to test her pussy.

He groaned when he discovered she was soaked and was about to penetrate her when Nic grabbed his shoulder, drawing his attention. He gave his friend a sheepish look when he saw the foil packet in his other hand and quickly suited up.

After donning the condom, he blanketed Joni's body and aligned his dick with her dripping cunt.

"This is going to be fast and hard, love," Tom whispered against her ear and then he sucked the lobe into his mouth and nipped on it.

"Oh," she moaned and then she groaned as he pressed into her with one long hard shove, until he couldn't go any farther.

"Fuck!" Tom held still as her tight cunt enveloped and clenched around his hard cock. He wanted to savor her heat, but he was so horny he couldn't remain still.

Joni whimpered as he withdrew and then sighed as he surged forward again. His pace was steady and he made sure that the head of his dick rubbed against her G-spot with each advance and retreat and, although she was moaning and gasping, it wasn't enough.

Tom wanted her insensate with hunger for him and he wanted her screaming his name. He shifted back until he was kneeling behind her and gripping her hips, with his upper body at a ninety degree angle with hers.

He nodded to Nic and Gabe to move in and they didn't hesitate. Gabe shifted until he was under her upper chest and started sucking on her nipples while Nic took her mouth.

Tom swore his eyes rolled back in his head as he pumped his hips, driving his cock in and out of her heated, moist pussy. It didn't matter that his breath sawed in and out of his lungs, or that sweat dripped down his face and filmed all over his body, what mattered was loving his woman. Making sure she enjoyed every millisecond of his lovemaking and that she climaxed before he did.

"I love the way you feel around me, Joni. You feel like ho…heaven."

Joni moaned as her pussy clenched around his dick and when Tom felt the beginning tingles at the base of his spine, he reached around and began to massage her clit. She mewled and whimpered as her juices flowed until they were dripping from his balls.

He could feel the tension invading her body and knew from her heavy breathing that she was right on the edge but as he fucked her harder, it wasn't quite enough. He released her hip, lifted his hand, and, as he withdrew until the tip of his dick was inside her tight cunt, he brought his hand down onto her ass hard.

"Come now, love," he ordered.

That was all it took. She screamed, "Tom," as her pussy grabbed hold of his cock before releasing, only to clamp down hard on him again. Tom drove into her twice more and then he shouted. His testes hardened as they drew up and then fire was rolling along the length of his dick as his seed shot out of him so hard he actually saw stars.

Load after load of cum expelled from his cock with the most forceful climax he'd ever experienced. His legs actually trembled and he swore he nearly blacked out as his balls felt like they turned inside out as they emptied. Each time he shot off her pussy gripped and milked more seed from his body.

When he finally had nothing left to give, he realized that he was collapsed on top of Joni, and that he was squishing her into the mattress. He had no idea when Nic and Gabe had moved away from their sub and didn't really care. He lifted up onto his elbows so he wasn't crushing Joni and sighed with relief when he heard her take a deep breath.

Her eyes were closed, but she had the most beautiful smile on her face, and although he'd never been a bragger, his heart filled with pride because he had put that smile on her face.

Joni was going to be their wife in the end and he wasn't going to let anything get in the way of that happening. Not even her.

* * * *

Joni had never felt so relaxed or so loved in her life.

She'd fallen asleep after Tom had made love to her and although she'd given Gabe a blowjob she still felt like she wasn't as connected to him as she was to Tom and Nic since they'd made love.

She woke up with him wrapped around her and Tom and Nic were missing from the bedroom. Yet she felt so safe and secure in his arms. In all of their arms. She was still in bed with Gabe spooning her and, even though she knew she should be getting up and readying herself for the work day, she didn't want to. Her career had been the be all and end all of her existence, but now she was beginning to rethink her goals. It wasn't that she wanted to quit, because she didn't, but she realized that all of her waking hours had been spent working with hardly any downtime to relax or play. Or to pursue her dream of becoming a full-time writer.

"Are you okay, sweetheart?"

That was another thing that amazed her. She hadn't moved a muscle but Gabe had known she was awake. It was like they could see into her soul and she wasn't sure how she felt about that.

She was still a little torn about what she was doing because although they got aroused around her and had told her she was beautiful, she had no idea how any of them felt about her. Did they care for her just because they were lusting after her? Or was it that they were just being compassionate and helped out anyone in trouble? Or was there more to it than that?

Nic had told her that if she agreed to making love with him, them, that she would be theirs, but for how long? Did they want a permanent relationship? Or was it only going to be a temporary thing, until they were tired of her?

"I'm fine."

"I can hear your mind working from here. Do you want to talk about what you're thinking so hard over?"

As much as she wanted to confront him, Nic, and Tom, she wasn't that brave. If she asked the question, she had to be prepared for the answer and she just wasn't ready to hear it yet.

"I need to get ready," she said and looked at him over her shoulder.

His jaw clenched and his lips pulled tight as if he were disappointed with her answer but he didn't press her. *Thank god.*

"Let me get the shower warmed up." Gabe kissed her shoulder and then he released her and rolled from the bed before heading into the bathroom.

Joni sighed and walked into the en suite. After using the facilities, which were thankfully behind a closed door, she moved to the shower. Gabe was already standing under the stream of water and held his hand out to her. She took it and stepped in, but when she reached for the shampoo he beat her to it.

"Turn around, sweetheart."

She did as she was told and blinked back tears when he soaked her hair and then began to wash it. The last time she'd had her hair washed was when she was a kid. Having his hands massaging her scalp and washing her tresses reminded her of what she'd lost.

She drew in a deep ragged breath and was glad that the tear which escaped her wouldn't be noticed because of the water from the shower. Joni stood still and enjoyed his hands moving over her body as he washed her.

When he was done, he turned her back to face him and rinsed off. She looked down when the head of his cock brushed her stomach and moaned when she saw how hard he was.

He wrapped an arm around her waist and pulled her into him, his erection pressing into her skin.

"I want to make love to you, Joni. Will you let me?"

"Please." She met his eyes and let him see how much she needed him.

He grasped both her hips and lifted her up against him, before turning her around to press her back against the cool tile wall.

"Wrap around me, sweetheart."

Joni had already looped her arms around his neck so she lifted her legs and hooked them around his waist and mewled when his cock rubbed against her pussy.

"Shit! Hang on a second." Gabe loosened his hold on her hips and then reached up to the shelf where she saw a small foil pack.

She nibbled on her lip as she debated whether to tell him that she was on the pill to regulate her menstrual cycle, but decided she wanted to wait until she trusted them a little more. It wasn't that she didn't trust them healthwise but she knew that contraception was never one hundred percent safe, and until she knew what they all wanted from her, she was going to bide her time.

Gabe had the condom on quickly and then he moved his hands down to her ass. He gripped her cheeks and lifted her a little higher and then he was sinking into her wet, needy pussy.

Joni's eyes rolled back in her head and her eyelids drifted closed as he stroked all the way into her.

"Look at me, Joni," Gabe demanded.

She forced her passion-heavy laden lids up and met his hungry green eyes.

"I want you looking at me while I make love to you, sweetheart."

Joni mewed with pleasure as he began to withdraw, but nodded her acquiescence of his directive, and then she moaned as he drove forward again.

With each pump of his hips he rocked harder and faster, pressing in deep and her blood began to heat. And as she stared into his eyes she was certain she saw more than lust as he watched her.

But then all thought fled and all she was able to do was feel. In and out his cock slid, faster and faster. His body slapped against hers and she clung to him with her arms and legs.

Her muscles grew taut and she gasped for each breath. The head of his cock was hitting that spot she'd only read and heard about and thought was a myth until these men. With each rub, the tension increased and she wondered how she was able to grip his hips with her legs when they were shaking so much.

Liquid desire heated her pussy, her womb, and then it was traversing her blood stream. The walls of her cunt gathered closer and closer, rippling around and gripping his cock as if it never wanted to let him go. And it didn't. She didn't.

She was in love with Gabe, Nic, and Tom and in that instant it didn't matter if they never loved her back. She would cherish this moment and the previous ones with Nic and Tom for many years to come no matter the outcome.

He shoved forward deep and fast and Joni cried out with bliss and the emotions overflowing her heart. And she was flying.

Flying high on nirvana as she climaxed. Flying high on love and happiness as she soared high above the clouds.

Just as her quaking cunt began to wane Gabe growled low in his throat as his green eyes hazed over and he surged deep. She moaned with joy when his cock jerked inside her pussy, enhancing the pleasurable aftershocks still quivering inside in answer to his climax.

When he stopped shuddering and trembling, he leaned down and kissed her. The kiss brought tears to her eyes because it was so reverent it almost felt as if he were worshipping her like he'd just worshipped her body.

He finally lifted his head and smiled at her as he lowered her feet back to the floor and her heart stuttered.

Would she be able to walk away if they grew tired of her?

No.

The answer shouted loudly through her mind and Joni hoped that this thing between them would work out, because she didn't think she'd be able to survive if it didn't.

Chapter Thirteen

The next week was gone in the blink of an eye. Joni was so happy she didn't think anything would be able to break into her euphoria. Nic and Gabe had gone back to their landscaping business full time and although they dropped into the hotel after they'd finished for the day, they left the management of the hotel to her. Tom was also back to his security job at the club.

This morning before they left for work Gabe had brought her a cup of coffee and they sat talking about their plans for the coming day and Nic had joined them. Tom had been in bed with her, cuddling up to her back and he'd woken when the other two had started talking to her.

After a quick glance around, she saw the lunchtime crowd had dwindled and the couple of people sharing drinks in the back corner still had full glasses so she let her mind drift back.

"We want to take you to the club tonight, sweetheart." Gabe reached over and took the empty coffee mug from her hand and put it on the bedside table. It was Friday and, although her heart rate picked up with excitement at the thought of going to that club with them, her job came first.

"Um…I have to work."

"You hired some good, reliable people. You don't need to hover over them all the time," Nic interjected. "I looked over the roster when we came in last night. You have more than enough staff rostered on to cover the Friday night crowd."

Joni wanted to say yes, but was still a little trepidatious about being naked in front of other people. What if Kara was there? Would she be able to look at her friend again knowing she'd seen her naked?

"What are you thinking about?" Tom asked in a sleep-rough voice.

"We've been training you in BDSM and you're taking to it like a duck to water. What has you hesitating?" Gabe asked.

"What if Kara's there?"

"What if she is?" Nic asked.

"She could see me."

"So? What's wrong with that?" Tom questioned as he shifted to a sitting position with his back against the headboard.

"I've never been naked in front of strangers before." Joni pulled her lower lip between her teeth.

"Do you have a problem with the way you look?" Gabe asked in a growly voice.

"No, but I don't know if I want my friend seeing me...so exposed."

"Okay. I can relate to that. We can always use one of the more private rooms off the great hall," Nic said.

Joni sighed with relief, some of the tension easing from her muscles. "Then I think I would like to go to the club with you."

Tom smiled at her. "Thank you, love. Your trust means a great deal."

"We have to go," Gabe stood up but then he kneeled on the floor right next to her. "Don't work too hard today. I don't want you wearing yourself out." He cupped her face between his hands, leaned forward, and kissed her passionately before getting up and walking out.

"See you tonight, baby." Nic walked closer, bent down, and kissed her hungrily, too, before he left.

"Why are you still holding back with us, Joni?" Tom turned to face her more directly.

Joni felt guilty about not telling them everything, but it had become second nature for her to not talk about her life. At least the painful personal stuff anyway. She wanted to tell them but she just couldn't make herself do it. She didn't want to see them looking at her with pity or horror over what her dad had done. Plus, she was scared she would end up like her father. As the saying went, the apple never fell far from the tree.

She still had no idea what these three gorgeous, confident, authoritative men wanted with her. She was a nobody, and they could have any woman they wanted with just the click of their fingers. What did they see in her? She wasn't model beautiful, she had a nice body, but so did a lot of other women?

"I..." She didn't know how to answer his question without giving too much away. It wasn't that she didn't trust them, because she did. She would never have let them make love with her if that were the case. And she knew they would never deliberately set out to hurt her, but in the end everyone who'd ever loved her had left and she wasn't sure she would be able to cope with the pain if they grew tired of her and asked her to leave.

Joni needed to hold some of herself back because it was the only way for her to survive.

"You know we'd never hurt you, right?"

She nodded. She didn't want to do this now. Didn't know how to explain without hurting him, so she decided it would be prudent to ignore the elephant in the room and get ready for her day. She rolled out of bed and headed to the bathroom. Joni cringed inside when she heard Tom's disappointed sigh and, when the door was closed behind her, sagged against it for a moment.

Why did she feel like she'd failed him, Nic, and Gabe? Why did she feel guilty when none of them had been forthcoming? Maybe she should just go back to her apartment and get on with her life.

"They'd probably be better off if they never met you, Joni. You're a fucking mess and you're only going to bring them down."

"Miss, are you okay?"

Joni came back to the present with a blink and hoped her face wasn't as red as it felt. She hoped the guy standing on the other side of the bar hadn't been there too long waiting for her acknowledgement.

"Sorry, just thinking about what I need to do tomorrow. What can I get you?"

Joni served him but gave him his drink on the house since he'd had to wait for her.

"Thanks. Are you sure you're all right?"

"I'm fine." She smiled and hoped he didn't notice that the smile wasn't genuine.

"Hey, would you like to go out one night?"

"Um…thanks but I'm already involved."

The good-looking guy gave her the once-over as he picked up his tray of drinks and half turned away. "Of course you are," she heard him mutter.

She was flattered, but he didn't do a thing for her and she suspected no one else ever would. Gabe, Nic, and Tom were it for her, but there was no way she would ever tell them that.

She'd been having the time of her life but knew it couldn't last. Nothing good in her life ever did. She'd learnt so much about their lifestyle but knew there was more she didn't know.

Her mind drifted back to the start of the week. Monday had been a slow day at the hotel and she'd closed up early. When she'd walked in the door all three of them were sitting on the sofa. Gabe had risen to his feet, spread his legs shoulder width apart, and crossed his arms over his chest. The heat in his eyes had almost singed her, but when he blinked it was like a cold mask had covered his face.

"Strip."

"What?"

He'd hurried over to her and gripped her upper arms, making her drop her purse on the floor. "Is that any way to address one of your

Doms? You've just racked up a punishment." He released her and eyed her coldly. "Remove your clothes. Now!"

Joni lifted shaky fingers to her shirt and began to undo the buttons. When she saw movement behind Gabe she noticed that Nic and Tom had moved to stand behind him. Her heart pounded in her chest and her breathing escalated until she was panting, but she lowered her head and did as she'd been told.

She shivered when the cool air wafted over her naked skin and goose bumps pebbled on her flesh but she kept her gaze lowered.

"Such a good little sub," Nic said as he moved around behind her. A shiver of desire raced up her spine when he caressed down her back, over her butt cheeks, before he gripped them in his hands. "You have such a sexy ass. I can't wait to fuck it."

Joni gasped and although she'd never even thought about anal sex, Nic's words were an erotic statement that had her body lighting up.

"She likes that idea," Tom said as he moved to stand closer.

"I think it's time to find out what else she likes." Gabe caressed a hand down her arm until he was clasping her hand. "Come."

She'd wanted to snap at him that she wasn't a damn dog, but when she peeked at him from beneath her eyelashes and saw the stern yet hungry look in his eyes, the words had caught in her throat. He'd led her back to that spare room with all the BDSM equipment.

"If you're going to be our sub then you need to learn how to act. Kneel," Gabe ordered pointing to the floor.

She looked down and was relieved to see a thin mat on the floor. With more haste than grace she knelt and clasped her hands in her lap.

"No. Not like that." Nic bent down and shifted her until her legs were spread with her ass resting on her heels. "Place your hands on your thighs palm up and keep your gaze on the floor."

"That's good, Joni. Remember that position because every time we tell you to strip this is what you'll do when you're naked," Gabe said.

"Stand up, sub," Tom ordered.

Joni wondered why they'd tell her to kneel if they were going to make her stand again but kept her mouth shut. She didn't want to rack up any more punishments. She was already nervous about what they were going to do to her for the other supposed infraction.

She got to her feet with as much dexterity as she could and stood with her head lowered waiting for their next order. She didn't want to admit it, but she was wet because their authority turned her on.

"Come here," Nic commanded.

She looked up to see him standing in front of that weird *X* thing and took a tentative step toward him.

Smack.

"When you're told to do something, you do it straight away," Tom said in a firm voice which surprised her because he always seemed to be the easier going of the three.

"Yes, sir," Joni replied and hurried over to Nic on shaky legs.

"Step up," Nic ordered and she took a deep breath before stepping up onto the padded step.

"Lean your front against the St. Andrew's Cross," Gabe ordered.

Joni held in her gasp when her naked skin met the cool padded *X* and hoped they couldn't see how much she wanted their touch.

"Grab hold of those rings and spread your legs," Nic said.

Again she did as she was told and bit her tongue to keep from protesting when they secured her to the contraption with cuffs around her wrists and legs.

"You're a good little sub, Joni. You please us when you obey," Tom praised.

Warmth filled her heart and she wondered why their approval meant so much to her.

"We are going to flog you, sub. If at any stage you get too scared or it's too much for you to endure, you will use your safe words." Nic moved around behind the cross, gripped her chin, and lifted her head so that she met his gaze. "What are your safe words, sub?"

"Y–yellow and red, sir."

"That's right. And what word do you use if you're comfortable with what's happening?" Gabe's breath wafted over her neck, making her shiver.

"G–green, sir."

"Good."

Nic leaned forward and placed a light kiss on her lips and then he was gone. She shivered with anxiety and excitement. Not sure whether she should be begging them to let her go or touch her.

Joni heard movement behind her and although she wanted to turn her head and look back over her shoulder to see what they were doing she remained still. When something slid over her head and then her eyes, she gasped and wanted to ask what was going on, but again remained silent.

"A blindfold will enhance all your other senses," Tom whispered in her ear. "I want you to try and relax and just feel. Okay?"

"I'll try, sir."

"Good girl."

Hands rubbed over her ass and then squeezed, shaping the globes, making more juices leak from her pussy onto her thighs.

Smack.

Her flesh heated and it was hard not to moan and beg for more.

Smack. Smack. Smack.

A whimper of need slipped from her mouth and she tried to shift but the restraints held her fast.

"Look at that nice pink ass," Gabe rasped. "You like having your ass spanked don't you, little sub?"

"Y–yes, sir."

"What do you do when given an order, sub?" Nic asked right before his hand slapped on her right ass cheek.

"Obey, sir."

"Good girl."

Smack.

"Look at that wet pussy," Tom rasped. "Our sub likes being controlled."

Smack.

"It's time to up the ante," Gabe said.

Joni shook with anticipation and desire. Her cunt clenched, her clit throbbed, and her nipples were so hard they were aching.

"I'm going to flog you, sub. Use your safe word if you need to," Nic said.

"Yes, sir."

Joni heard the swish of tendrils right before they landed on her ass. It was really hard to stay still and not press her hips back into the flogger.

"Count them out for me, Joni."

"One."

Smack.

"One what?" Gabe barked out his question.

"One, sir."

"You please me, sub. We'll start over," Nic said before the tendrils hit her ass again.

"One, sir."

"Good."

Another hit with the flogger. This time on the other ass cheek.

"Two, sir."

Joni continued to count out each swish of the flogger against her skin. Every inch of her back, ass, and legs was hot from being hit except for her kidney area. By the time she counted to thirty she was shaking but not with fear. She trembled with a hunger so great she wasn't sure she could take much more without begging them to fuck her.

Her womb ached with need. Her pussy throbbed with each beat of her heart and she was so wet from the cream dripping down almost to her knees.

"How are you feeling, sub?" Tom asked.

"Green, sir," she answered.

She was so high with adrenaline and need she wasn't sure she would be able to stay on her feet. And then she moaned. Fingers caressed the length of her pussy, spreading her juices but not once did they go near her clit.

"Do you like being submissive to us, Joni?" Gabe asked.

She nibbled on her bottom lip before answering. If she told them she did would they want to control her all the time?

Smack.

She gasped and groaned. Her ass was on fire but the hard smack of the hand on her heated skin just seemed to ramp her arousal up even more.

"I asked you a question, sub. Answer me, now!"

"Yes, sir."

"Good girl. I would have known you were lying if you'd said no, but you need to tell me what went through your head when I asked that question."

"Will…"—she paused to lick her dry lips—"will you want to order me around all the time? Sir?"

"We already told you that we only want to be dominant over you in the bedroom and in play," Nic said. "We're not like that fucker, sub. Don't insult me by thinking we are."

Tears filled her eyes. She knew she was being unfair to them and although she trusted them, it was hard to let go of her fear since she held onto it for so long. "S–sorry, sir."

"You don't need to be sorry." Gabe sounded frustrated. "You just need to trust that we will never hurt you, but you also need to be rewarded for being honest. Make her come, Tom."

Joni drew a deep breath and exhaled raggedly when Tom's fingers pressed up into her sopping pussy. She wanted to buck her hips and draw him in deeper, but knew if she moved he'd probably back off. She wasn't sure she could stand much more of this so she drew on all of her reserves and stayed still.

"Good girl." Tom kissed one ass cheek and then the other. "I know you wanted to move. You need to trust that we will always give you what you need."

She groaned when he added a third finger and then he began to pump them in and out of her hard and fast. Her wet cunt made squelching sounds, which would have embarrassed her if she wasn't so horny, but all thoughts drifted away and all she could do was feel.

Joni felt like she was an ephemeral being, floating on a cloud of desire so intense she didn't think she'd ever feel whole again. Each time he stroked into her, the pads of his fingers hit the trigger hidden inside and then he added a thumb to the mix. His thumb brushed over her engorged sensitive clit as he pressed in deeply and then she was screaming.

Her scream was so loud it hurt her throat but she couldn't seem to stop. Her whole body shuddered, her pussy clenched and let go, and then cum gushed out in a great wave of release. She saw stars and could barely draw a breath as her juices continued to flow from her body, dripping down her legs onto the step and floor.

Joni had never come so hard in her life and knew in that moment she was deeply in love with the three men. She was ruined for anyone else. They had taken her to a level of arousal she knew no one else ever could take her to. But it wasn't all about lust and sex, at least not for her.

But did they have feelings for her? Did they just want her because they wanted to fuck her for a while and when they were done, would they drop her on the wayside and never look back?

What have you done, Joni?

You should have run fast and far while you had the chance.

Chapter Fourteen

Joni couldn't stop the feeling that she was being watched. She would be glad when she could leave and hurry home so she could get ready to go out to the club. Every time she felt eyes on her she looked around but could never see anyone watching her beyond a glance, but she just couldn't shake the feeling that she was being stalked.

When she glanced at the clock she realized it was time to go. She looked over to Michelle, one of the casual bar staff, and then to Greg and saw that they were handling the demand for drinks well.

"I have to get going," she said to Michelle as she handed change over to a customer.

"Have a great night."

"Thank you. Call if you need me."

"We'll be fine. The people in here are patient and nice. We won't have any problems."

"Okay. See you on Monday."

"That we will. You deserve some down time. You work way too hard."

Joni shrugged but smiled and waved before heading out. She stopped into the office to grab her purse and shut down the computer before she locked the door and headed to the rear exit.

Nic was supposed to pick her up and because she couldn't get rid of the creepy feeling of being watched, she hoped he was waiting for her. She glanced about when she got outside and sighed with relief when she saw him leaning against his truck.

He stood up straight and hurried over to her. "What's wrong?"

"Nothing."

"Are you sure? You look a little…scared."

"I'm fine."

"Okay." Nic opened the door for her and then lifted her in before racing around to the driver's seat. "Are you nervous about tonight?"

Fuck yes. "A little."

"You have nothing to be scared about, baby."

So you say. You're not the one with the crumbling walls falling from around your heart.

"I know."

"You'll enjoy it, Joni. Haven't we shown you how good BDSM can be?"

How can I say no when he's right? "Yes."

"Just trust us, baby. We only have your best interests at heart. You know we won't hurt you."

"Yeah, I know." She sighed because she knew that they would never hurt her on purpose. The ride home seemed to be over much faster than normal and she hurried to the shower. Joni wanted to be smooth and clean for the play scene she knew they were going to do tonight.

She hoped she was doing the right thing. Her mind was in turmoil, but her body and heart seemed to be jumping a jig of excitement. But what worried her was how Gabe, Tom, and Nic seemed to be able to get her to spill her guts. She'd told them about Angus nearly at the start but she didn't want them to know about how her father had left her and then came back years later to kill her mom.

She had a feeling that if she ever spoke of that horrific time in her life that she would break and never get herself back. There always seemed to be a knot of terror lodged in her heart but she'd pushed it down deep and tried to keep it there. But sometimes the memories came to the surface and no matter how hard she tried to box them up again, they wouldn't be contained. When that happened she usually sequestered herself in her apartment and cried for hours on end before drinking herself into oblivion. She never drunk any other time because she'd seen the affect alcohol had and didn't like the way people lost their inhibitions and behaved in ways they wouldn't normally.

Would she end up crazy like her father? That was her deepest fear and, although she'd spoken to her counselor about that terror and been told the likelihood of that happening was about a million to one, she just couldn't let the fear go.

Joni stepped into the bedroom with a towel wrapped around her and stopped when she saw Gabe sitting on the edge of the bed.

He pointed beside him. "This is what we want you to wear tonight. Nothing else. Do you understand, little sub?"

"Yes, sir."

"Good. Be ready in ten minutes." He rose to his feet and after giving her a pointed look as if to reiterate his command, he left.

Joni picked up the top and frowned when she saw it was a corset-looking thing with hooks down the front. It was blue and black and felt soft in her hands. With another sigh of resignation she dropped the towel and put the top on. She picked up the leather-type black skirt and pulled it on over her hips. She guessed she wasn't getting any underwear to wear since none was laid out. After quickly braiding her hair, she held onto the wall and slipped her feet into the stiletto-style shoes.

She was ready to go and no doubt was running out of time. She glanced in the mirror and froze when she saw herself. The outfit formed to her curves like a second skin but she was surprised that she liked the way she looked wearing it. It made her feel sexy and feminine and the heels made her legs look much longer than they were. She just hoped she didn't break her neck trying to walk on them. She'd never worn anything so high before.

When she heard voices coming from the living room, she drew in a deep breath, pushed her shoulders back, and headed out.

She just hoped she wasn't making a big mistake by agreeing to go to their club.

* * * *

Gabe was anxious to get the night started. This was the night they were going to get Joni to open up to them fully. They'd spent the last week training and easing her into BDSM and she'd responded beautifully. But he and his friends were sick of her holding back with them.

He knew she trusted them because he could see it in her eyes, but that wasn't all they could see. She had no idea that when she looked at them that they could see how much she loved them. He, Nic, and Tom loved her just as much, if not more, but she wasn't ready to hear it yet. They'd shown her in so many ways how they felt but she still had a wall around her heart and wasn't seeing.

All of that ended tonight. They were going to send her into subspace and get to the crux of her fears. She needed to purge whatever was holding her back before they could move forward, and move forward they would. Failing wasn't an option. He loved her so damn much, he wanted to collar her and then ask her to marry them.

He looked up when she tottered down the hall toward them. His breath caught in his throat and his heart stuttered when he saw how fucking beautiful and sexy she was. When she looked at each of them her eyes softened and the love shone out, but he wasn't sure if she even realized what she felt. She would before this night was over. He wasn't letting her hide from them anymore.

And once they got her to open up he and his friends would reveal their love for her, too. She needed to hear what they wanted from her besides the physical aspect of their relationship. He'd often caught her watching them with a frown on her face and worry in her eyes as if she were trying to work out what their angle was.

Tonight was the night she would stop hiding. He couldn't wait to make love to her with his friends. They'd been holding that back from her but had prepared her for it. He, Nic, and Tom had decided that they would only make love to her together when she knew how much they loved her. They didn't just want their joining to be about lust, they wanted it to be about the emotions, too.

"Ready?" he asked as he held his hand out to her.

"Yes," she answered softly and put her hand in his. So much trust without any equivocal hesitation.

"Let's go." Nic nodded and headed out with Tom on his heels.

Gabe guided her to the garage and helped her into the backseat of the truck. He held her hand and, although she remained quiet on the drive to the club, he knew she was nervous. Her palm was sweaty and, even though she tried not to fidget, she was restless.

When they arrived he lifted her out and wrapped an arm around her waist to keep her steady. "Remember the rules, little sub. Keep your head down and don't speak unless asked a question. Okay?"

"Yes, sir."

"Good girl." He led her up the steps and introduced her to Aurora and Tank.

Aurora explained the club rules to her and then gave her the documents to sign. Joni read over them quickly, inhaled deeply, and then signed on the dotted line.

"Have a good night," Aurora called out and Joni was about to reply but a stern look from Gabe had her clamping her lips tight.

"Good girl."

"Sir, may I have permission to ask a question?"

"Very pretty, Joni," Nic said as he paused at the closed double doors to the club interior. "Ask."

"Is Kara going to be here?"

Gabe almost smiled at the nervous squeak in her voice, but held it in. "Yes, but we've asked that her Doms keep her away from you tonight. And don't think that will happen all the time, sub. You're going to have to get over your aversion to being naked in front of people you know and seeing them naked, but we'll give you a little more time."

"Thank you, sirs." She sighed with relief and some of the tension in her shoulders diminished.

Nic opened the doors and took one of her hands in his. Gabe kept his arm around her waist and Tom walked behind her. All three of them knew how important this night was and the determined sparkle in their eyes belied their nervousness.

They didn't have to speak to know that everything was on the line, but Gabe and his friends were determined to come out on top. Losing wasn't an option.

He stopped outside one of the semiprivate rooms. "Wait here, sub."

Gabe walked into the room and made sure that everything was set up the way he wanted. They planned on some bondage with impact play and wax play. When he saw everything they needed was here, he motioned Nic and Tom to bring her in.

"Strip!"

He kept his eyes on her as his friends moved to stand beside him and was pleased when she did as he'd ordered, again without hesitation.

"I'm very happy with you, sub," Gabe praised and knew his praise had pleased her by the slight blush to her cheeks.

"Come here, Joni," Tom demanded as he moved to the spanking bench and she walked over to him. "Kneel on the step and put your hands here."

Again she complied with Tom's commands.

Gabe walked to her head and secured her wrists to the hooks after enfolding her skin with the fur-lined cuffs while Nic and Tom wrapped the large straps over her thighs, restraining her so she couldn't move.

"Do you remember your safe words, sub?" Nic asked.

"Yes, sir."

"Go through them for me," Tom said.

"Green, yellow, and red, sir."

"Good girl," Gabe praised and caressed his hands over her shoulders and down her back. "Hmm, you're nice and relaxed. You trust us to take care of you, don't you, Joni."

"Yes, sir."

"Good." Gabe moved away so she couldn't see him but made sure he could see her. He needed to keep his attention on her to make sure they didn't go too far. If they did that, he knew they were lose her completely. He took a deep breath to calm his racing heart and nodded to Tom to begin.

* * * *

Tom massaged and kneaded Joni's ass before caressing his way up her back to warm her skin. He was going to spank her but didn't want to start out cold and damage her beautiful, soft skin. When he felt she was warm enough he smacked first one ass cheek and then the other.

She remained still and quiet but as he continued to spank her ass he hit harder and harder. When he counted fifteen smacks to each buttock, he stepped back to admire her pink skin and was glad to see she was breathing heavily. His cock was so fucking hard, all he wanted to do was strip off and plunge into her wet cunt, but this was about more than sex and he wasn't going to do anything to ruin their chances of a long, lasting relationship with the woman he loved.

"How are you feeling, sub?"

"Green, sir."

"Good girl." He moved closer again and grabbed her ass cheeks lightly, pleased when she moaned. Her pussy was glistening with dew and her thighs were wet.

"Did you like my hand smacking your pretty ass, sub?"

"Yes, sir."

"Then you're going to love what Nic does next." Tom nodded at Nic and moved around so he could see Joni's face. Her face was flushed, her eyes were closed, and there was a dreamy smile on her face, but he could tell by her fast aroused breathing she wasn't anywhere near subspace yet.

Nic grabbed the paddle off the small table off to the side and then walked toward Joni. He smoothed it over her ass. "Do you know what I'm going to do to you, sub?"

"No, sir."

"I'm going to paddle your ass and you are going to love every minute of that, aren't you, Joni?" Nic asked in a gravelly voice.

Tom met his eyes and nodded to let him know that Joni was on board with what he'd said. Her face was a pinker hue and her nipples engorged even more.

"Yes, sir."

* * * *

"Good, sub," Nic said before he slammed the paddle onto her ass. He kept his eyes on her body, watching her body language as well as taking cues from Tom. This was about Joni, not him, or Gabe and Tom. This was about freeing her from the walls she constricted around herself and, hopefully, by the time they'd finished with her she wouldn't hold back with them anymore. He and his friends wanted her flying free so she could love them like she needed and they could love her right back. Not that he didn't love her already, because he did with his whole heart, but this relationship wouldn't work the way things stood.

He wanted the whole nine yards with her. Wanted to marry her and have kids with her. Nic kept paddling her ass and by the time he reached thirty-five he wasn't sure she was going to reach subspace.

Gabe moved to stand beside Tom but made sure to keep out of her line of sight. When Gabe and Tom gave him the thumbs-up at the same time he knew she was getting close.

"Now, Gabe," Nic said.

Gabe stepped to Joni's side, knelt down, and began to rub her clit. She moaned and gasped and tried to arch up, but couldn't since she was restrained. Her skin was coated with a light sheen of sweat and her pussy was dripping wet.

"Two more," Tom murmured.

Nic pounded on her ass twice more and then stopped. He hurried to her side and looked at her face. The muscles in her face were relaxed as if she were asleep but he knew she was hyperaware of every move he and his friends made. His muscles and body was pumped with adrenaline and was in a heightened state of arousal and awareness, too, and, as much as he wanted to fuck her with his friends, they needed to get answers from her.

"Joni, why do you keep your heart closed off?" Nic asked softly, not wanting to break her out of the semitrance she was in.

"Hurts, so much," she slurred.

"What hurts, sub?" Tom asked as he squatted down in front of her.

"When everyone…leaves."

"Who left you, sweetheart?" Gabe asked.

"Father," she sobbed. "He left me. He killed her."

"Who killed who?"

"Dad, left, long…ago. Came back," she sobbed. "Years. Ran over my mom."

Nic wanted to roar with anger at the pain he could hear in her voice, but he held it in. He took a deep breath and then asked his next question.

"Do you think it was your fault you dad left?"

"Yes. Naughty girl."

"Fuck!" Gabe muttered.

"How old were you, Joni?" Tom asked.

"Eight."

"You were just a little girl. Your father leaving had nothing to do with you, love."

"He was crazy. He came back after years of being gone, hunted my mom down, and ran her over with his car." Joni sobbed and Nic's heart ached and filled with anger as well. He'd bet his last dollar that was when the asshole, Peace, had found her.

"I'm sorry," Gabe said as he began to undo the restraints around her thighs and Tom worked on the wrist cuffs.

"What if I end up crazy like him? I don't want to love anyone, it hurts too much." She started sobbing uncontrollably and Nic scooped her up into arms and held her tight. "I can't tell you how much I love you all. You'll get tired of me and then where will I be?"

Nic's heart ached for the wealth of pain she'd kept trapped inside of her heart. She was sobbing so hard her whole body was jerking and shuddering. Gabe hurried across the room, grabbed a blanket, and wrapped it around her naked body. Tom hurried from the room and came back a few minutes later with Turner in tow.

"What's going on?"

Nic could hear Tom explaining to Turner but didn't look up from Joni. He hated that she was crying so hard and hoped they hadn't killed any chances they had with her, by what could be considered as using subterfuge.

"Bring her to the guest room," Turner said before turning on his heel and leading the way.

Nic's eyes burned with unshed tears as Joni continued to cry. He was worried she was going to make herself ill. He followed after Gabe and Tom, down the glassed-in hall, to the far door leading to Turner's private quarters.

He entered the room and rushed over to the large bed where he laid down, spooning himself around Joni.

Her tears had lightened up a little but her head and body were jerking with shuddering hiccups.

"Shh, it's all right, baby. Don't cry anymore. You're breaking my heart."

Finally her tears ceased but then the shakes began. He knew it was because she was coming down from being so emotionally overwrought as well as the endorphins from being in subspace.

"I'm sorry, Joni," Tom said in a hoarse voice as he climbed on the bed next to her and stroked a hand over her head.

Gabe got onto the bed near her feet and placed his hand on her leg, rubbing up and down to offer her comfort.

Nic nodded his thanks to Turner when he walked out, closing the door behind him.

"I know it's probably the last thing you want to do right now, baby, but you need to tell us what happened. There's poison inside you that needs to come out."

Joni shook her head and drew in a deep, ragged breath before exhaling gustily.

"I already…told you." She hiccupped and pressed her body back into Nic's seeking his warmth.

"I–I…Can I have some water?"

"Shit! Sorry, sweetheart." Gabe hurried to the kitchen, grabbed a bottle of water from the fridge, rushed back to the bed, and then handed it to Joni.

"You need to tell us, love." Tom helped her sit up and Nic shifted until he was sitting beside her. He slung an arm over her shoulders and pulled her into his side, being careful not to jostle her as she drank deeply.

"My dad left my mom and me when I was eight. For the longest time I thought it was because I'd been naughty. It didn't matter that my mom had told me that it wasn't my fault. You know how kids are and I remember I'd been a brat the day he left, so it just sort of made sense to self-blame.

"It wasn't until years later that my mom explained that my dad had become verbally abusive and he'd hit her. Apparently I witnessed that but I'd somehow managed to block the incident out.

"Anyway he was gone and I never saw him again. The day after I turned twenty I was waiting for my mom to come home from work. I had dinner already cooked and kept it on low to keep it warm. She was late but I figured that she'd been kept back at work."

Nic took the empty water bottle from her and placed it on the bedside table.

"I waited for two hours. When the knock came at the door I thought it was my mother and she'd forgotten her keys. I was smiling and was about to tease her, but when I opened the door and saw the policemen on the doorstep...I knew something dreadful had happened.

"They informed me that my mom had been involved in a hit-and-run accident and even though they were looking for the driver, they hadn't been able to find him yet." Joni paused to wipe a hand over her face.

"I had to go down to the morgue and identify her body for their records.

"It took them six weeks for the police to find all the evidence and by then my father, who had managed to escape the mental hospital he'd been institutionalized in, was back where he should never have been able to break out from."

"God, sweetheart, I'm so sorry." Gabe leaned over, snagged her around the waist, and pulled her into his lap. "I know how much that hurt you. To have your father kill your mom like that, but do you really think your mother would want you to hold yourself back and not live? Don't you think she'd want you to be happy, to find love and live a full life?"

"I don't know if I can. What if I allow myself to love and it's not returned? I don't think I could deal with that sort of heartache again."

"Love is scary," Gabe began. "I got engaged right after finishing high school. I was young and full of life with the whole world in front of me. I had been dating Sonja since middle school. We were going to get married and start a family early.

"I'd just met Nic and Tom when I started working at a security company. Sonja was commuting to college, studying to become a nurse. We were going to be married in three months' time."

Joni reached out and took Gabe's hand in hers.

"She'd just come out of college and was walking toward the parking lot to her car. She never made it. Some fucked up ex-student decided he was going to take out as many students as he could before turning the gun on himself."

"Oh, Gabe. I'm so sorry."

"You have nothing to be sorry for, sweetheart, and, although I grieved and felt guilty for a longtime after Sonja died, it wasn't because I felt like any of what happened to her was my fault. Do you know why I felt guilty?"

"Because you were alive and she wasn't."

"Yes. It took me a long time to get my head out of my ass and realize that she would have been angry with me. I was a mess. I was existing and not living at all. If it hadn't been for Tom and Nic, I don't know if I would be here right now. But I'm so glad I am because I would have missed out on meeting you.

"You are a very special person, Joni Meeks. You are beautiful inside and out and I love you very, very, much."

Chapter Fifteen

Joni felt like she'd been pulled through a wringer backward. At first she'd been horrified and then embarrassed by her breakdown, but once her tears had slowed, the pain and grief she'd been carrying around for so long lifted and she felt lighter than she'd ever felt in her whole life.

Her heart had ached for Gabe when he told her about his fiancée but she was at a loss for words with his declaration of love. She'd never expected to hear those words from any man.

"I…"

"My turn." Tom clasped her hips and lifted her to his lap. "I know it doesn't help to hear these words and you'll always have a huge hole in your heart from losing your mother and, even if you don't admit it, your father, too. But be thankful you had time with both of them even if it wasn't a lifetime.

"I have no idea who my parents are, love. I was found in a box dumped on the steps of a church, and spent my whole life in the foster system. You've known what love felt like and, although I have these two idiots, it's not the same as having parents or a partner. Yes, I love Nic and Gabe like brothers but that pales in comparison to the real thing.

"I've been with a lot of women and even had a relationship or two, if you could call them that, but those relationships were based on lust and not love. They were doomed from the start. I never knew what it was to truly love someone until I met you. I love you, Joni Meeks." Tom leaned down and lingeringly kissed Joni on the lips.

Joni's heart began to fill with joy until it felt like it was overflowing. She opened her mouth to tell them all that she loved them, too, but Nic reached over and placed a finger on her lips to halt her, and then he cupped her face between his hands.

"My sister died when she was ten. My mom had gone over next door to help an elderly neighbor and since our dad walked out when I was a baby, there was no one to watch over us.

"Vanessa was two years older than I was and was supposed to keep an eye on me but I didn't want a girl watching me, because at that age girls had germs. I went to my room to play.

"If I'd been with her, maybe Vanessa would still be alive, but I'm not sure. A car came around the corner too fast and lost control. It ended up in our living room where Vanessa had been playing with her dolls. She was killed instantly."

"Oh, god," Joni sobbed and grabbed hold of Nic's wrists. "You probably would have ended up dead, too."

"Maybe. I grieved and blamed myself for not being there with her. It took me a while to figure out that we had no idea what fate would bring us and we can't control every aspect of life. If I had been in the living room and died with her, my mother would have been alone and I know she wouldn't have been able to have born the guilt of losing both her children at the same time. She was a shell of herself after Vanessa was killed and, although she went through life as best she could, she was never the same. She died a couple of years ago when she got pneumonia and, even though she never said it, right before she died I saw relief in her eyes. Relief from the guilt and pain of being with a neighbor and not with her kids when her daughter was killed.

"I loved her as much as I could and hoped she'd let the survivor's guilt go. If she'd done that she might very well have found love again and lived a long full life. But it wasn't to be.

"I vowed then when I found love that I was going to reach out and grab and hold on tight with both hands. There are no guarantees in anything, but to live life in fear of losing isn't living at all.

"I love you, Joni Meeks. You are everything to me."

Although she was already in love with them, she felt herself fall in that moment, all the more for them. Her heart was so full of happiness and love she was almost bursting with it and couldn't contain the emotions anymore.

"At first I thought you only wanted me for the sex." She held up a hand when all three opened their mouths as if to refute her statement. "Please, let me finish. It's my turn."

Nic was holding one of her hands as was Gabe. She was still sitting on Tom's lap and she loved how protected and cherished she felt with them surrounding her with their bodies and heat.

"Go ahead, baby." Nic squeezed her hand with encouragement.

"I knew as soon as we made love for the first time I was in trouble." She paused to lick her lips. "No, actually that's a lie. I knew before I even turned to look at you when we were at the club the first time that you were a threat. Everywhere you touched me with your eyes tingled. But I wasn't ready for you then and the only thing I could do was run."

"We knew you were attracted to us, sweetheart." Gabe lifted her hand to his lips and kissed the back of it.

"Yeah, well, I didn't like the way you made me feel. I'd vowed after Angus to never get involved with another man again. Having the three of you pursuing me was terrifying, but I needed to work and thought I could keep the attraction locked down tight."

"We were determined, love." Tom hugged her tighter for a moment.

"Yes, you were. Dogged is more like." She smiled. "Little by little you worked your way into my heart and I just couldn't seem to walk away. I wanted to. I tried, but you made me feel so special.

"I want to thank you all for not giving up on me. I'd lived with that pain for so long, I wasn't sure I would ever feel…normal again. But you three are like my knights in shining armor and were relentless in breaking down those walls I had." Joni drew a deep breath and cupped Tom's face between her hands.

"I love you, Thomas Quentin. Thank you for helping to set me free." Joni leaned forward and kissed him. It wasn't a carnally passionate kiss, but she made sure to portray every ounce of love she felt for him into it. When she released his lips, she was surprised and humbled to see he had tears in his eyes. He opened his mouth but snapped it shut as if not knowing what to say, or too overcome with emotion to speak, and then he smiled and nodded at her.

Joni crawled from Tom's lap over and onto Gabe's. She sighed with joy when his arms wrapped around her body and she was safe with the knowledge that these men would never, ever hurt her. She gripped his shoulders and stared deeply into his beautiful eyes.

"I love you, Gabe Solar. Thank you for your love and care and for helping me to live again."

"You're very welcome, sweetheart. I would do anything for you." Gabe was the one to lean down and kiss her. This kiss was more passionate than the one she'd shared with Tom, but was also full of love and emotion. When they pulled back she was the one with tears in her eyes and rolling down her cheeks.

She wiped her face with the back of her hands and just as she was about to crawl over to Nic, he grasped her hips and lifted her over to him.

"Thank you for helping me to fly free, Nicholas Flange. Without you all I would still be hiding from the world. I love you so much, Nic."

"You're my heart, Joni. There's nothing I won't do for you."

"Good. I want to go home."

"Your wish is our command, sweetheart. That is unless we're in the bedroom or doing a scene with you." Gabe grinned and waggled his eyebrows and they all burst out laughing.

She dressed quickly, a little disappointed that they hadn't gotten to make love to her, but they had the rest of the night to do so and she wanted to be in their home, in their bed when they did. Although she loved the club and was eager to come back for some more carnal delight, she didn't want anyone seeing them while they made love after they'd all declared their love for each other.

She wanted to savor their touches, kisses, and loving in the privacy of their home, because to her this was a very special moment.

Nic pulled her into his side when she was dressed and they exited the room back into the noisy, yet highly erotic, atmosphere from the club.

"Do you want to come back?" Gabe asked as he drew up to her other side.

"Oh, hell yes."

"That's great, love," Tom said from behind her. "We still have so much to show you."

"I'm looking forward to it. Just not tonight."

"We understand, baby." Nic leaned down and kissed the top of her head as he guided her to the double ornate timber doors. "We are going to spend the rest of the night making love to you and we're all going to love you together."

Joni's heart thumped with excitement. "Promise?" she asked in a breathy voice.

"Fuck yes, sweetheart."

Joni giggled as they walked outside and rushed toward the truck. She was so full of excitement and anticipation she didn't notice the man leaning against the vehicle until it was too late.

The excitement waned and in its place fear erupted, until her legs were trembling and she felt as weak as a baby.

Paul, a neighbor she'd barely exchanged a "hi" with, stood in front of them with two guns, one in each hand and they were pointed at her and her men.

"Paul? What are you doing?"

"You know this man, Joni?" Gabe asked in an angry voice.

"H–he's a n–neighbor."

"Why didn't you come to me?" Paul yelled his question, spittle flying from his lips.

"What? What are you talking about?"

"You were supposed to come to me when your place was trashed. You were supposed to seek me out when you got scared."

"Uh…I'm sorry…"

"Shut the fuck up. You're a slut just like the rest of them. I've been watching you for months. You were supposed to be mine. I knew I had to do something when I saw the way you looked at them."

Joni shivered. She was so scared but she was more worried that one of her men was going to get shot. Maybe if she kept him talking it would buy them some time. Hopefully whoever was watching the security monitors could see that they were in trouble.

"How could I be yours? We hardly acknowledged each other?"

"Joni," Tom grabbed her hips and pulled her back a couple of steps.

"Don't move," Paul roared and pointed one of the guns at her head.

Her body shook so bad and her mind raced as she tried to think what to do. No matter what scenario crossed her mind, she discarded it. Even if she was able to distract him, she knew she would end up getting shot, but so could one of her guys. That thought was unacceptable to her. She loved them more than her own life and would do anything to make sure they stayed safe.

"What do you want from me?" Joni was surprised at how calm her voice sounded, when she was quaking with fear.

"You. I want you, Joni. You were supposed to love me." Paul's shoulders slumped and the guns waivered.

She pulled from Tom's grip and held up her hands when Nic and Gabe grabbed for her arms and rushed forward a few steps.

"Joni, what the fuck are you doing?" Nic asked in a low, angry voice.

She gave a slight shake of her head and placed one hand behind her back, shaping her finger and thumb hoping they understood she wanted them to call 9-1-1 on their cell phones.

As she moved closer, she saw a couple of shadows moving in toward Paul from behind him and nearly sighed with relief. She wasn't out of the woods yet, but if she kept him looking at her, whoever was creeping up on them might be able to get the jump on him.

"Did I ever give you the impression I was interested in you?" Joni cringed at her question and the anger she heard in her own voice. She didn't want to incite him, but she just couldn't seem to help herself.

She'd just found the love of her dreams and she wasn't letting him take that away from her.

"You saw me watching you," Paul snarled. "I know you did."

"And when I did see you I said hello. Did it ever occur to you that if you were interested in dating me, to ask me out?"

"You wouldn't have given me the time of day. I watched you. You never even noticed when other men looked at you. Not until you started working for those assholes."

"So what do you want me to do? I'm not going to lie to you. You can't make someone love you, Paul. It doesn't work that way."

Without any warning Paul lunged for her. He used her body as a shield, holding one of the guns against her temple as he dragged her sideways. That was when she heard sirens in the distance and knew the police were on their way.

"Turn around and say good-bye, Joni. You're coming with me."

"Let me go. Please? You won't get away with this. The police are already on their way."

Joni reached up to push the gun from her head but froze when she heard him cock it. She looked over to Nic, Gabe, and Tom, meeting each of their gazes through her tear-filled blurry eyes.

I love you all, Joni mouthed as tears streamed down her face. She prayed that the men who had been creeping up on Paul made their move soon, but she wasn't sure they would get to her in time, because he was keeping his back to the vehicles as he dragged her with him.

And then everything seemed to be moving in slow motion. Someone jumped down on top of her and Paul and a loud bang sounded in her ears, making them ring. White-hot agonizing pain seared her upper arm and then it went blessedly numb. Another gunshot rang out and then another. She fell to the ground and Paul fell on top of her, his dead weight making it hard to breathe.

Spots formed in front of her eyes, but when she inhaled she couldn't draw any air into her lungs and she gave in to the darkness.

Chapter Sixteen

Tom had never been so scared in his life when he saw the guy pointing the guns toward them. He wasn't scared for himself but was terrified Joni would be taken from them before they could really start their life together.

His first instinct was to pull his own gun, but he wasn't on duty and hadn't brought it with him.

When the guy started ranting at Joni that she was supposed to be with him, Tom nearly lost it. But that was nothing compared to the fear and anger racing through him when she pulled away from them and walked toward the fucker with the guns.

Since the perp couldn't look at all of them at the same time, he slowly and carefully pulled his cell phone from his pocket and dialed the surveillance room. Hopefully, whoever was in there was watching the horrifying scene unfold and had already called the cops.

He nearly sagged with relief when he saw one of his colleagues trying to sneak up behind the fucker that was now using Joni as a shield. When he glanced to the side he saw another man moving in and his heart nearly stopped beating altogether. He had no idea who he was and he didn't have a gun, but he was worried he was there to help Joni's neighbor steal her out from underneath their noses.

But when the older guy climbed up onto the roof of a truck and placed his fingers over his lips, his knees almost gave out. He wasn't here to help hurt their woman, he was trying to help save her.

And then everything seemed to happen at once. The guy on the roof of the truck leapt off and as he landed on Paul's back, he reached for the gun.

Three shots were fired almost simultaneously and he stumbled as he raced toward Joni as she went falling to the ground. The Paul guy had fallen on top of his woman and as he hauled him off of her, he looked over to see that the older man was also on the ground with a gunshot wound to the chest.

Gabe and Nic were kneeling over him trying to stem the flow of blood pouring out of the hole in his chest.

"Call the paramedics," Tom yelled. "She's been shot."

He ripped his shirt off, wadded it up, and pressed the material against her bloody upper arm. Although he was aware of more people milling around, he only had eyes for Joni. She looked so small, fragile, and pale, but she was breathing deeply and evenly.

"Tell her," the older man gasped and coughed and Tom knew when blood came out of his mouth that he wasn't going to make it. "Tell her...I'm sorry. Sick. Didn't...know...what...I...doing."

"Who are you?" Gabe asked as he pressed down harder on the man's wound.

"Father," he gasped out before he stopped breathing.

Paramedics arrived and though they tried to revive him, there was nothing they could do.

Tom watched as another medic assessed Joni and, after wrapping her arm, loaded her onto a gurney and wheeled her toward an ambulance. He raced after them, not willing to leave her until she opened her pretty blue eyes and looked at him again. He climbed in the back of the van and, after finding what hospital they were going to, yelled it out to Gabe and Nic, knowing they would be held up for a while dealing with the police.

He sat by her head, stroking her hair out of her face, and willed her to wake up.

The paramedic looked up at him. "She'll be fine. It was a through shot and as far as I can tell no arteries or bone was hit."

Relief coursed through him that she was going to be okay, but he wouldn't believe she was out of danger until she was smiling.

It seemed to take forever before they reached the hospital and he rushed to the emergency room only to be told he couldn't go in. He paced back and forth for over two hours, looking up each time the doors opened, only to be frustrated when he was ignored.

"Tom!" Gabe called out and he looked up to see him and Nic almost running down the hall toward him.

"How is she?" Nic asked.

"I'm still waiting."

"Fuck!" Gabe spun away before turning back.

"The paramedic said he didn't think any arteries or bone got hit by the bullet and that she should be fine."

Nic grabbed onto his shoulder as if he couldn't hold himself up anymore and then he seemed to gather himself and straightened when the double doors opened.

"Are you here for Joni Meeks?"

"Yes," Tom said as he moved forward with his hand out.

"I'm Dr. Watson."

Tom introduced himself and his friends.

"Joni is going to be fine. She has some muscle damage which will leave her sore and in need of rehabilitation but she will have full use of her arm."

"Thank god," Gabe muttered.

"When can she go home?" Nic asked.

"We've stitched her up and given her a shot of antibiotics and painkillers and she'll be a bit drowsy for a few hours, but she can go home in an hour or so. We just need to make sure she doesn't have any adverse effects to the medication."

"Thank you so much, doctor." Tom shook his hand again. "Can we please see her?"

"Sure, a nurse will be out in a few minutes to take you back. She'll need to see her GP to get the stitches out in seven days and make sure she takes the course of antibiotics so infection doesn't set in. I've written out a prescription for some pain medication and suggest you fill it at the hospital pharmacy before you leave. Other than that you'll be good to go in about an hour."

"Thank you," Gabe and Nic said before they both shook the doctor's hand.

Ten minutes later, a nurse came out to lead them to their woman.

* * * *

Joni ached from head to toe and frowned when she heard noises she'd normally hear in a hospital. She tried to remember what happened but her mind was foggy.

"She looks so pale," Nic said in a hoarse voice.

Joni forced her heavy eyelids open to see Nic, Gabe, and Tom all frowning with worry.

"Joni, how are you feeling, love?" Tom asked as he moved to the chair at her bedside and sat before taking her hand into his.

And just like that she remembered her neighbor, Paul, holding a gun to her head. She bolted upright and cried out when her arm began to throb.

"Shh, sweetheart. You're safe. Lie back down." Gabe hurried to the other side of the bed and sat on the edge.

Tom sat near her feet and placed his hand on her shin over the blanket.

"He shot me, didn't he?"

"Yes," Tom answered.

"What the hell were you thinking?" Nic asked angrily. "You could have been fucking killed."

Tears welled and trickled down her face. "I'm sorry. I just wanted to make sure none of you were hurt. I've only just found you."

"Don't cry, love," Tom said and glared at Nic.

"I'm sorry, baby," Nic apologized. "I didn't mean to yell at you, but you scared the hell out of me."

"All of us," Gabe said.

"Did anyone get hurt?"

Gabe looked at Nic and then glanced over at Tom. Tom frowned as if he didn't know what was going on before meeting Gabe's eyes again.

"Tell me," she ordered and tried not to moan in pain when she moved her injured arm.

"You should be resting, sweetheart," Gabe hedged.

The door opened before she could reply and Detective Gary Wade walked in.

"How are you feeling, Joni?"

"Okay," she lied but knew from the looks her men gave her that she would pay for that later.

"I need to take your statement. Are you up to it?"

Joni wasn't feeling well at all but she just wanted it all to be over so she gritted her teeth and nodded her head. After taking a deep breath she told him what had happened.

"Thank you. I hope you feel better soon," Gary said and turned toward the door.

"Wait! What happened to Paul?"

"Uh, he died at the scene."

"How?" she asked. She could tell they were holding something back from her and, even though dread knotted in her stomach, she needed to know.

Gary walked back to the bed and sighed.

"Joni," Nic paused and squeezed her hand.

"Just tell me."

"Your father managed to escape from the mental hospital a few weeks ago. At first we thought he was the one who'd trashed your apartment. Gary and the police have been looking for him but he managed to stay hidden."

Joni covered her mouth as she gasped with fear.

"You're safe, love. We've got you." Tom got up on the bed and carefully maneuvered them both until she was leaning against him and she was wrapped in his arms.

"I don't how he came to be there but your father saved you, baby," Nic said.

"He was the one who jumped Paul and fought for the gun," Gabe explained. "He took a bullet in the chest trying to help you."

Joni didn't know what to say, so she remained silent. She'd loved her dad before he left, but after he'd killed her mother she'd been so angry and full of hate she didn't know how to feel. "He died, didn't he?"

"Yes, baby. I'm sorry."

She felt horrible because she didn't feel anything. Maybe she was just too numb to feel, or maybe it was because the pain medication was kicking in and she was feeling a little woozy. Or maybe it was because he'd taken away something very precious from her and she just couldn't find it in her heart to forgive him.

Nic cleared his throat. "He said to tell you he was sorry, that he was sick and didn't know what he was doing."

Joni nodded and wiped her face when she felt moisture trickle from her chin. She hadn't even realized she was crying.

"Are you all right, love?" Tom asked.

"Yes," she slurred and her eyelids began to droop. "I thought I hated him, but I don't. Life's too short to hold in so much pain and anger. It only makes you bitter and wrecks things. I forgive you, Daddy."

Joni slumped against Tom with a lighter heart and knew that everything was going to be fine.

Chapter Seventeen

Joni was so excited, she was buzzing inside. Her men were taking her to the club tonight and she couldn't wait.

It had been two weeks since she'd been shot and although her arm had healed she was still going through rehab. Her men had hired another bar manager and although she'd planned to go back to work when she had the all clear from doctor she was beginning to reassess her goals. She wanted to talk to her men, but had to get things in order in her own mind before she told them what she wanted.

Gabe was beginning to get annoyed with her because he, Nic, and Tom often caught her staring off into space while she'd tried to decide what she wanted to do with the rest of her life, careerwise. Of course, she kept telling them there was nothing wrong and changed the subject, but she could tell they weren't going to put up with her evasiveness for much longer.

"Are you ready, love?" Tom asked as he entered the bedroom.

"Yes."

Fifteen or so minutes later, she was being led into the Club of Dominance. The sounds of sex, pain, and pleasure made her pussy clench and moisten, and her imagination went off on a tangent as she tried to imagine what they would do to her.

"Joni, I'm glad to see you."

Joni looked up to see Masters Turner and Barry smiling at her with their wife sub Charlie standing between them. They had visited her at home while she'd been recuperating.

"Thank you, sir."

"You're getting the hang of it." Charlie smiled and then rolled her eyes when Master Barry swatted her ass.

"Do you have permission to speak, little sub?" Master Barry asked in a hard voice.

Joni shivered but was thankful these two intimidating men weren't her masters. They looked so cold when chastising their sub.

"Oh, bite me." Charlie stuck her tongue out but winked at Joni.

"Oh, you are just racking up the punishments, sub."

"Goody." Charlie smirked but then she squealed when Master Barry bent over, pushed his shoulder into Charlie's stomach, and lifted her off her feet.

"Enjoy your evening." Master Turner smiled. "I know we will."

Joni chuckled when she realized that Charlie had been goading her Doms into punishing her and wondered if it would work for her, too.

"Don't even think about it," Gabe said as he met her eyes.

"It got her what she obviously wanted," Joni said.

"You don't need to go to such drastic measures, baby. All you have to do is ask," Nic said and waggled his eyebrows.

"But that wouldn't be as much fun."

"She's right," Tom said and before she could blink he lifted her from her feet and up over his shoulder.

"Put me down." Joni wiggled, but froze and gasped when a hard slap landed on her ass.

"Joni, how are you doing?" Kara asked.

Joni pressed her hands against Tom's back and lifted her upper body slightly so she could see her friend.

"I'm great. When are we going to do lunch again?"

"Next Friday," Kara nearly yelled her answer since Tom was carrying her away. "I'll call you."

"Tom."

Smack.

"What did you call me?" Tom asked in a hard voice and Joni knew the scene had started.

"Sir, that was rude."

"I don't care. You can talk to Kara anytime. This is our time."

Joni slumped over him with a happy sigh, because he was right. This was their time.

She teetered on her feet when he lowered her to the ground, but he held her hips until she was steady before he released her and stepped back. After a quick glance, she sighed with relief when she saw they were in one of the semiprivate rooms. She just wasn't into exhibitionism and was glad her Doms weren't making her stand naked on that stage out in the great room.

"Strip and kneel, sub," Nic ordered.

Joni quickly removed the bustier and short skirt before placing them neatly over a chair and nudged her shoes beneath it.

"Good girl." Nic moved behind her and caressed her skin from the top of her shoulders to her ass. He paused and kneaded her buttocks before swatting her lightly. "Get up on the table on your back, baby."

She hurried to do his bidding, surreptitiously trying to see what Gabe and Tom were up to. She bit her tongue to hold in a moan of desire when Nic slapped her thigh. "Eyes down, sub."

With a sigh, she lowered her eyes, still trying to peek, but she couldn't see anything. Then her eyes were covered with a blindfold and all her other senses ramped up. She could hear her own blood rushing through her veins near her ears and it felt like her whole body was moving with every beat of her heart. Goose bumps rose up on her flesh, her nipples hardened, and her cunt throbbed.

"Someone's excited," Gabe said and then hands were brushing against her legs as they were restrained.

She shivered when Nic caressed her inner wrists as he tethered them and then sighed when his lips met hers. She melted into the padded table beneath her as her hunger for her men grew.

"Have you ever heard of wax play, baby?" Nic asked after he released her lips.

"N–no, sir," she answered tentatively.

"You have nothing to be scared of, sub," Tom said, his voice close.

"Do you trust us, Joni?" Gabe asked.

"Yes, sir," she answered immediately and sincerely.

"Good girl," Nic praised. "Just remember to use your safe words if you need to."

Warm, moist hands landed on her shoulders and began to caress all over her body. She couldn't help but moan when they ran over her breasts, kneading and cupping the globes. She whimpered when her nipples were squeezed and plucked and smiled when she heard Gabe chuckle. More hands touched her hips and she groaned as they smoothed all over her lower abdomen, wishing they would go lower where she was aching to be touched.

"We're coating your skin in oil, love," Tom explained. "This will make it easier to get the dried wax off later."

"Hmm," she hummed and luxuriated in the sensation of their touch.

She was so hungry for them, but wasn't sure she would have them all loving her tonight. She needed them all so badly but kept her mouth shut in case she racked up any punishments. One thing Joni had learned about herself with these men was she hated to disappoint them. She liked it when they were happy with her and complimented her for her good behavior. If anyone had told her three months ago she would be laying her throat bare to three men, she would have laughed in their face. But the truth was she felt so fulfilled and free when they were controlling her body and she loved every minute of it.

"Are you ready, love?" Tom asked.

"Yes, sir."

"Such a polite response," Nic said. "We love how courteous you are, baby."

"Thank you, sir."

"My pleasure, Joni." Nic's hands cupped her breasts and tweaked her aching nipples in reward and she couldn't contain her whimper of need.

"Soon, sweetheart," Gabe said. "Once we've finished with this scene, we're all going to love you like you've never been loved before."

Joni remained silent since she wasn't supposed to say anything unless she was asked a direct question but she wanted to beg them to love her now.

She gasped when hot wax landed on her stomach and although it was very warm, it didn't burn her skin. With each drop of melted wax on her body, she seemed to relax more and more until she felt like she was floating on a cloud.

All her senses were heightened and she knew where each of her Doms were by scent alone. She didn't need her eyes to know that Nic was standing on her right side dripping wax on that half of her body, or that Gabe was standing to her left doing the same.

Tom was standing near her feet and drizzling hot wax up and down her spread legs and the higher he got the more her clit throbbed, her pussy clenched, and cream wept from her cunt. She wanted to arch her hips up in silent supplication for the next touch but didn't want them to stop so she remained still.

Although her body was relaxed, she was hyperaware of everything and could smell the musky scent of her men's arousal and the paraffin in the unscented candles. Joni moaned when wax was dripped onto her breasts and she willed Nic and Gabe to move that heat to her nipples.

But they seemed intent on teasing her, keeping her on edge with the anticipation and excitement of not knowing where the wax would land next. Her whole body quivered with need when Tom drizzled the warm stuff on her totally nude mound—Gabe had ordered her to remain hair free for all of their pleasure and she was so glad she had complied—and she couldn't help but try to bow her hips up.

And then she cried out when a slap landed on her pussy right over her swollen, needy clit. The sting made her gasp and juices leaked from her cunt as it clenched, but it wasn't enough to send her over. That slap had just seemed to ramp up her hunger that much more and it took her a couple of moments to notice she was sobbing form the pleasurable pain.

"Don't move again, little sub, or everything will stop. Do you understand?" Tom asked in such a cold voice tears burned her eyes at disappointing him.

"Yes, sir." Her reply was almost incomprehensible. Her tongue felt like it was moving too slow and almost cleaving to the roof of her mouth. But she was in awe of the breathy quality of her voice because she sounded almost like she was in a dreamy trance.

And then she realized that was exactly what she was experiencing. She was super attuned to everything her Doms were doing, but so relaxed she felt like she was floating. Her men had done what she thought of as the impossible. They had sent her into subspace. As that knowledge floated across her mind she recalled being here once before, when they had broken down the armor around her heart and gotten them to talk about her father.

And then all thought fled.

Another moan left her mouth when the hot wax plopped onto both nipples simultaneously and she whimpered as Tom licked her cunt from her ass to her clit and back again. It felt like cream was almost pouring out of her in such copious amounts, it made her womb ache. But it wasn't a bad pain. It was so good she wanted to be filled in every hole just like she'd imagined her men doing time and again.

Tom dripped the wax onto her pussy lips and she tensed with expected eagerness of it hitting her clit, hoping it wouldn't be too hot and burn her delicate skin.

And just as she began to relax when that drip didn't occur, something plopped right on top of her engorged pearl and she cried out as her euphoria consumed her entire existence. Her whole body trembled, her pussy contracting in waves of nirvana as she flew so high she could barely breathe.

Just as she thought the climax was going to wane Tom shoved two fingers deep into her cunt and curled them up, rubbing right over her G-spot. The climax intensified, making her shake and shudder with ecstatic jubilation, cum expelling from her in a great gush.

Joni didn't know if she'd blacked out or just continued floating on rapture but when she became aware of her surroundings once more, she was curled up in Nic's arms and he caressed a hand up and down her back as he whispered nonsensical words to her.

She licked dry lips and pushed up into a more upright position and when a bottle of water was held against her lips, she drank greedily. She hadn't even realized the wax had been cleaned off, but her men had taken great care of her. She could smell the scent of a light moisturizer on her skin. Her whole body felt soft and satisfied.

"How are you feeling, baby?" Nic asked in a deep, raspy voice and when she met his eyes she could see the hunger in them. His hard cock pulsed beneath one of her ass cheeks and she felt him tremble slightly.

"I feel wonderful," she replied in a quiet, awestruck voice. And she was awed at how much they could make her feel. "I love you, Nic."

"I love you, Joni."

"I love you, Gabe, Tom."

"We love you, too, love," Tom called out.

"Are you ready for more?" Gabe walked over from where he and Tom had been cleaning the equipment with disinfectant and he stroked a hand over her head before leaning down and kissing her on the cheek.

"Are we going home?"

"Do you want to?" Tom asked as he moved closer.

When she looked at each of her guys it looked like they were hanging on by a thread. Their muscles were pumped with blood and their sinews were standing out in stark relief and in that moment her satisfied libido kicked into high gear.

"No. I want you all to make love to me."

"Here?" Gabe raised an eyebrow as if surprised by her request.

"Yes. Please?" Joni didn't care who saw them, all she cared about was having them touching her, loving her.

"Let's move," Tom said before turning and leading the way from the room.

Chapter Eighteen

Nic could barely stand, let alone walk, he was so hungry for their woman, but he shifted his hold on her and followed Tom to Turner's private rooms.

Gabe had asked that they be able to use the guest room after scening with Joni and he'd agreed. Nic was so happy about that right now because he leaked pre-cum and his balls were aching so much they almost hurt.

When he entered the room, he hurried over to the bed and gently lowered her. He was still pumped with adrenaline after sending their sub into subspace and making her scream her lungs out as they made her come. She was so beautiful, his heart hurt just looking at her, but seeing her cry out her pleasure would be forever etched into his mind.

Joni trusted them completely and all the walls she'd had up for so long were gone. She submitted so beautifully.

He and his friends had been longing for this moment and he had every intention of making sure she enjoyed having the three of them loving her at the same time, she would beg them to do it over and over again.

Nic stripped his clothes off quickly and then he crawled up onto the bed next to her. Tom and Gabe were still undressing so he leaned up and began kissing her, stroking her body and flicking her nipples with his thumbs.

He broke the kiss when Tom and Gabe got onto the bed, Gabe on his back next to Joni and Tom remained on the bottom as he waited for them to situate their sub. Nic helped her sit up, and then grasped her hips and lifted her up and over Gabe, so she was straddling his hips.

"Take me inside, Joni," Gabe demanded in a deep, husky voice.

Joni reached behind her, clasped the base of Gabe's cock, pressed it against her entrance, and then slowly sank down.

"Fuck!" Gabe gasped. "You're so hot, tight, and wet."

Joni moaned and began to lift up and down until she had all of Gabe deep inside her pussy.

"I'm going to fuck your ass, baby." Nic walked around behind her and knelt between her and Gabe's spread legs. He took the tube of lube Tom handed him, squirted some onto his fingers, and began to caress her anus.

Joni moaned and she responded beautifully to their previous anal play. Her ass opened to let him in and he pushed two fingers into her rear entrance, coating her tight channel with the lube.

"Do you like that, love?" Tom asked as he moved to her side. "Do you like having a cock in your cunt and fingers up your ass?"

"Yes. Oh."

Nic ground his teeth when her muscles clenched down at Tom's dirty words and when they relaxed again he added a third finger. He thrust them in and out of her ass a few times and then withdrew them again. He grabbed a condom, coated it with lube, and aligned his aching cock to her entrance.

"Take a deep breath, little sub. When you exhale, push back against me." Nic had no idea how he was able to talk coherently when he was shaking like a leaf with desire, but was glad he'd been so eloquent.

He pressed gently yet firmly against her rosette, his groan joining her moan as the head of his cock popped through the tight sphincter muscles, and even though his instincts were to surge into her all the way, he held still, giving her body time to adjust to his penetration.

"Please, sirs?" she gasped out between panted breaths.

"Please what?" Gabe asked.

"I want more. Please?"

Nic couldn't remain still any longer. His cock was throbbing right along with his heartbeat. He pressed forward another inch, drew back slightly, and as he surged forward again, she opened right up and he slid home.

"Fucking amazing," he groaned. "You submit so perfectly, baby."

"Look at me, Joni," Tom demanded in a firm yet breathy voice, showing he was just as hungry for their sub.

Joni pushed up on Gabe's chest with her hands, her internal muscles clenching around his cock as she moved and then she turned her head to see Tom on his knees, his fist wrapped around the base of his cock, waiting for her.

She didn't wait to be told what to do. Their little sub leaned over slightly and licked the tip of Tom's dick. She must have liked the taste of his pre-cum because she made a humming sound and then she swirled her tongue around the crown before sucking him deeper into her mouth.

"Fuck yeah, love. That feels so good," Tom panted.

Nic met Gabe's eyes and at his friends nod he drew out of her ass and as he pushed back in, Gabe withdrew from her cunt.

Joni moaned and hummed as she began to bob up and down Tom's cock and they all began to move in sync.

With each thrust of their hips, Nic and Gabe sped up their momentum until their bodies were slapping against hers. She was so fucking wet, her pussy made sloshing sounds, which turned him on even more.

She kept pace with them, moving her mouth up and down the length of Tom's cock. When Nic felt the warm tingle form at the base of his spine he knew he wasn't going to last much longer. Reaching around with one hand, he cupped a breast and then pinched and plucked at her nipples, alternately.

"I'm not gonna last," Tom rasped. "Her mouth is fucking amazing."

"So is her pussy," Gabe almost growled the words, his voice deeper than usual with desire.

"Her ass is so fucking tight." Nic drove deep before retreating again.

"I'm so damn close," Tom panted.

"Send her over," Nic ordered.

Gabe moved his hand and, from the way Joni's muscles clenched down and she moaned, he was rubbing her clit.

He surged into her harder, faster, and deeper. Heat spread from his lower back around to his groin, making his balls pull up tighter to his body.

"Joni!" Tom roared and then Nic heard her gulping down Tom's cum.

When Tom pulled from her mouth he collapsed onto the bed with an arm over his eyes, and Joni hummed with pleasure as she licked her lips.

And then she was keening. A deep guttural sound as she drew closer to climax.

Nic nodded to Gabe as he pulled back until the tip of his cock was just inside her ass, and then Gabe nodded. They surged in together as Gabe pinched her clit and she screamed.

Her internal muscles grabbed around his gliding dick before releasing and clenching again.

Fire surged into his balls, up his shaft, and he roared with pleasure. His cock shot load after load of cum into the condom. His whole body shook and shuddered, his dick twitching and jerking as he ejaculated like he'd never ejaculated before.

He heard Gabe yell and, as he came down from the most powerful climax he'd ever had, he realized Joni was slumped down on top of Gabe and he was slumped over her. He hadn't even noticed he'd moved.

With a gentleness he never knew he had, he eased his deflating cock from Joni's ass and knelt on the bed as he regained his breath and his equilibrium. Gabe rolled to his side, taking Joni with him, and he brushed the hair off of her face.

Her eyes were closed, her face and chest flushed and she had the most beautiful serene smile on her face. Her lids lifted and he could see the love she felt for them lighting her up with an inner glow.

"I love you, all so much," she sobbed with emotion. "Thank you all for not giving up on me. Thank you for making me live again."

"I love you, baby." Nic leaned forward and kissed her shoulder.

"I love you, sweetheart." Gabe hugged her tight and kissed her head.

"I love you, Joni." Tom caressed her ass.

"How about we clean up and go get a drink?" Gabe suggested.

"Yes," Joni replied. "Wait! I want to talk to you for a moment."

"What's up?" Nic asked.

"I want to become a fulltime writer." She nibbled on her lip and looked into each of their eyes. "But if you will allow it, I would also like to buy into the pub?"

Nic smiled. "That's great, baby, because we were going to ask you if you wanted to become a partner."

"You were?"

"Yes," Gabe replied with a smile.

"We want you to be happy, love," Tom said. "And we will support you in anything you want to do."

"Thank you," she whispered and sniffed when moisture filled her eyes.

"You're welcome, love." Tom nudged her toward the door. "Now, let's go get that drink."

* * * *

Joni and her men sat at the bar, sipping on their drinks talking to Kara, Nat, and Nixon.

The club was still full and the sounds she'd once found intriguing yet terrifying, now seemed normal. Two Doms and a sub had just finished an impact scene on the raised stage and, after cleaning the equipment down, left the dais.

The music cut off and then Gabe was taking her glass of wine from her hand and placing it on the bar.

He and Tom each took one of her hands in hers and Nic took the lead as they guided her through the crowd. Her heartbeat ratcheted up when she realized they were leading her to the stage. If they'd done this to her a few weeks back she would have balked but she knew they would never betray her trust by making her do something she didn't want to. Plus, she loved and trusted them unequivocally.

She walked up the steps and was glad Gabe was still holding her hand when she wobbled in the impossibly high heels.

Her men guided her to the front of the platform and then they turned so they were side on to the crowd. She turned to face them and was pleased that she no longer felt self-conscious in front of so many people.

Gabe cleared his throat and put his hand in his pocket and then all three of them knelt down in front of her. Her breath hitched in her throat and tears burned the back of her eyes but she kept the moisture wanting to form at bay.

"Joni, would you do us the honor of being our permanent sub?"

A joyous smile formed across her lips and face. "Yes. It would be my honor."

Gabe stood, pulled his hand from his pocket, and stepped forward. His hands brushed against the skin of her neck, making her shiver, and he smiled at her, his eyes heating with passion. She felt cool metal wrap her throat and then he stepped back.

The tears of happiness tracked down her cheeks as she realized they'd just collared her. Nic and Tom both reached out and clasped one of her hands in one of theirs, drawing her attention.

"Joni, would you do us the honor of becoming our wife?" Tom asked.

She sobbed as the tears flowed faster and opened her mouth to answer but she couldn't get the words out of her constricted throat. She nodded enthusiastically and then finally managed to answer. "Yes."

Nic and Tom stood and when she felt something being slipped onto her left ring finger she looked down and gasped. A large, square diamond with smaller baguette diamonds around the platinum band graced the ring finger.

She smiled through her tears, tugged her hands from theirs, and then threw herself at each of them, kissing them one after the other and then she laughed with joy. She was so intent on her guys she was only barely aware of the crowd clapping, cheering, and whistling.

Joni had never imagined she could love so hard or be so happy. She'd never have guessed that she was submissive or enjoyed BDSM and would never have had the chance to know or feel so much if it weren't for Gabe, Nic, and Tom.

Their persistence had paid off and she was so glad they hadn't given up on her. She was soaring free, flying high on love, life, and happiness and she had her three Doms to thank for that.

She was going to spend the rest of her life showing them just how thankful she was.

THE END

BECCAVAN-EROTICROMANCE.COM

ABOUT THE AUTHOR

My name is Becca Van. I live in Australia with my wonderful hubby of many years, as well as my two children.

I read my first romance, which I found in the school library, at the age of thirteen and haven't stopped reading them since. It is so wonderful to know that love is still alive and strong when there seems to be so much conflict in the world.

I dreamed of writing my own book one day but, unfortunately, didn't follow my dream for many years. But once I started I knew writing was what I wanted to continue doing.

I love to escape from the world and curl up with a good romance, to see how the characters unfold and conflict is dealt with. I have read many books and love all facets of the romance genre, from historical to erotic romance. I am a sucker for a happy ending.

For all titles by Becca Van, please visit
www.bookstrand.com/becca-van

Siren Publishing, Inc.
www.SirenPublishing.com

Lightning Source UK Ltd.
Milton Keynes UK
UKOW06f1847030815

256316UK00014B/598/P

9 781632 596499